Broken Windows

Patricia Nolan

Broken Windows
Stories

PATRICIA NOLAN

POLESTAR
BOOK PUBLISHERS

BROKEN WINDOWS
Copyright © 1996 by Patricia Nolan

No part of this publication may be reproduced, stored in a retrieval system or transmitted, in any form or by any means, without prior permission of the publisher or, in case of photocopying or other reprographic copying, a licence from CANCOPY (Canadian Copyright Licensing Agency), 6 Adelaide Street East, Suite 900, Toronto, Ontario, M5C 1H6.

The publisher would like to thank the Canada Council, the British Columbia Ministry of Small Business, Tourism and Culture, and the Department of Canadian Heritage for their ongoing financial assistance.

Cover photograph by Andrea Lowe
Cover design by Val Speidel
Author photograph by Katarina Cheslova
Edited by Brenda Brooks
Printed and bound in Canada

CANADIAN CATALOGUING IN PUBLICATION DATA
Nolan, Patricia, 1961-
      Broken windows
ISBN 1-896095-20-8
I. Title.
PS8577.O52B76 1996   C813',54   C96-910415-4
PR9199.3N64B76 1996

POLESTAR BOOK PUBLISHERS
1011 COMMERCIAL DRIVE, SECOND FLOOR
VANCOUVER, BC
CANADA   V5L 3X1
(604) 251-9718

10 9 8 7 6 5 4 3 2 1

For Don

I wish to express my thanks for funding given me by the Regional Municipality of Ottawa-Carleton, the Ontario Arts Council, and the Jack Hodgins Scholarship.

Some of these stories appeared previously in different form: "To Kingdom Come" (as "Beware of Dog") in *The Malahat Review*, "Hugging The Urn" in *Prism International*, "October Water" (as "Brooms") in *Grain*, "Chocolate Rosebuds" (as "Part Of My Story About Choclate Rosebuds" in *Quarry*, "In The Time It Takes To Breathe" in *The Malahat Review*, "Celestial Names" (as "Consider Me Gone") in *Canadian Fiction Magazine*, "Like A Bride's Nightie in *95: Best Canadian Stories*, "Mary with the Cool Shades" in *University of Windsor Review*.

Many thanks to my editor, Brenda Brooks, for helping me to see what was there. For providing me with a healthy balance of encouragement and skepticism, I am privileged to have met and worked with writers at The Sage Hill Writing Experience and The Ottawa Writers' Group. For words above and beyond the call of duty, I especially thank Diane Vist, Nadine McInnes, Robert Currie, Chetan Rajani, Mary Borsky, Janice Kulyk Keefer and Douglas Glover.

Broken Windows

To Kingdom Come ... *9*

Hugging The Urn ... *23*

The Simple Life ... *35*

Chocolate Rosebuds ... *51*

Broken Windows ... *57*

Mary With The Cool Shades ... *75*

Her Industry Of Lies ... *85*

October Water ... *93*

In the Time It Takes to Breathe ... *103*

Celestial Names ... *111*

Like A Bride's Nightie ... *125*

Drama Junkies ... *137*

To Kingdom Come

NONE OF THE NEIGHBOURS HAD SPOTTED JOHANNE'S DAD, or caught sight of any dog for the week and a half the sign had been in the window. Except for Alice Wilson. Rumour had it that when Alice allowed her poodle out to piddle at four o'clock one morning, she had spied Johanne's father tromping in and out of his back door clad in galoshes and boxer shorts, tossing pot after blackened pot into the snow — dishes, forks and knives as well. He pitched everything carelessly, but the knives were aimed at the trunk of the hydro pole. He karate-kicked the air after each throw. Blood was beginning to seep through a white band tied around his head.

"Joseph! What in Heaven's name's going on?" Alice Wilson called.

He disappeared and returned with a stack of his wife's good china — Fine Arts Rose. Each plate flew over Alice's fence like a frisbee. Her dog yapped and yapped, leaping to snag a plate between its teeth, darting away just in time to avoid getting knocked in the mouth.

"Never too late to have a happy childhood," Joseph sang. "I'm goin' crazy, Alice. Wanna come?"

❖

Johanne knew the orangey letters of the BEWARE OF DOG sign in the window were the kind that would glow in the dark. Being eleven and her younger sister nine, she knew they could sneak in the house by the sliding windows when her dad locked them out. Also, and probably, there was no dog.

Johanne and Julia, instead of heading directly to their grandmother's apartment after school, took little detours by their own house on Emperor Avenue. They climbed fences, pushed through cedars double their height and thickness, trudged through many backyards of snow. They walked with their backs pressed to the sides of their friends' houses, peeking from their friends' laneways, or even from behind their own snowbanks if they felt brave, peeking at the little bungalow with the crazy sign in the window. Often their friends were playing street hockey right in front of the house — Johanne suspected they didn't have their hearts in the game, they just wanted to see if all that stuff about Mr. Hamilton was true.

If their friends caught them, that would be *one* thing. If their dad did, he'd drag them in the house by the scruff of their necks and then stab them right through the eyes. Thinking about that would cut Johanne's spying short, would send her racing to the bathroom. Johanne could sprint faster when she had to pee than at any other time. Her sister would just wet her pants if she felt like it and then want to dilly-dally. Johanne, being the oldest, would have to slow down and, very parent-like, bark an order to hurry up.

"C'mon," she'd hiss. "You want him to catch us? You want to wind up at your own funeral?"

❖

To wind up at your own funeral was the worse thing Johanne could imagine. Her father had always done stuff — she was used to that — but this time, he'd gone farther. About as far as you could go, she suspected, before things had gone too far.

Johanne and Julia had been down in the rec room, pretending to do homework, really calling their dad names and inventing swear words. Their sneakiness, as always, made them giddy.

"Jesus Christhole. Fucking bastfrigger. Godfucked arsepicker."

Upstairs their mother screamed and they stopped laughing.

A few minutes later she stomped furiously down the stairs to fetch dry clothes for herself out of the laundry room. Whereas her Harlequin Romance — *Love Is Forever* — was curling at the corners, her wet hair was plastered, straighter and darker than usual, to her head. She undressed right in front of them. Nipples Johanne had never seen before poked out with goose pimples on them. White wiggly lines slithered over her mother's belly.

A bucket flew down the chute, crashed against the open hamper, bounced off. Her mother stood facing them in an orange sweater, a triangle of black hair. Then she sat, bare-bottomed, on the cold grey floor and began to laugh. Neither girl had ever seen that before either.

"Yoo-hoo!" Joseph called from the bathroom at the top of the chute. "Oh, Nora!"

Johanne looked up and started to cry. Julia, like her mother, was laughing.

❖

Joseph's head dangled from the chute, his shoulders poking out, the wood creaking. His body inched its way down and crashed first on the hamper, then on the floor. The thump of weight and bone on cement rendered him still, rendered them all still.

"Please be dead. Please be dead," Johanne whispered to her sister. Her father just lay there, eyes and mouth closed and deadly still.

Nora spun them around, ordered them upstairs with a sharp nudge. The two girls turned the corner, continued to watch as their mother tiptoed toward the heap, calling out his name.

"Joseph? Joseph? Are you dead?"

When she stopped within a foot of him, he whipped his hand around her ankle and pulled himself halfway up, onto an elbow. With his other hand, he presented her with a stiff bouquet of steak knives. In a second she kicked him where it counted. The knives scattered over a drainpipe in a pick-up-stick pattern and he drew up his knees like a wounded child, or a child about to throw a fit.

"Run!" Johanne yelled. Joseph was moaning now.

Johanne was first up the stairs, taking them two at a time. Nora came next, then Julia, dawdling. Johanne slammed the door and wedged a kitchen chair under the doorknob.

Her mother said, "Stay here, right here. I'm just going to the bedroom to grab a pair of slacks."

The telephone book lay open at the yellow pages, a butcher knife stabbed to an advertisement for taxis. The fan above the stove spun like an airplane propeller. The wind blowing through the blades reminded Johanne of wolves howling on a mountaintop. Of coyotes, or hyenas. A half-empty jar of hot banana peppers stood on the front burner, the burner behind it glowing orange.

"Fuckaduck friggers," Julia whimpered, "I forgot Cornelius."

Before Johanne thought to stop her, her sister had tossed the chair aside and rushed down into the basement.

❖

The police told Nora she'd have to be the one to break the little window and reach in to unlock the front door. They handed her a shovel from the car port. So as not to be called useless again, Johanne boastfully informed the officers that the shovel was a spade, used widely in the digging of graves. Her mother bashed the glass and stepped out of the way.

The outside light went on, although most of its brightness was absorbed by the officers' tall, bulky bodies. From behind they looked outlined and haloed in silvery blue; their breath curled into the air like furnace smoke from the rooftops.

Joseph answered the door, calm and polite. If he hadn't been standing casually on broken glass in his bare feet, Nora would have had a tough time convincing the police that this was the lunatic holding Julia inside.

"Out of the way, Sir," said one of the men.

"You can't come in here," Joseph said. "This is a private home. *My* home. Do you have a warrant?"

The other officer stepped in, eased his arm around Joseph, buddy-like, and led him into the kitchen. "How's about a nice cup of coffee, Mr. Hamilton?" he said, rubbing his hands together, blowing on them. "It's cold as a bitch out there tonight."

Johanne sped down the hall after her mother, to the back bedroom, which had belonged to her before she'd been permitted one downstairs. It had taken her a year's pleading and a year's allowance to be moved away from the rest of them.

Her sister was asleep with Cornelius. The lamb was pinned under her head like a pillow so he'd be there when she woke up. At one time she would have slept with him nestled beside her in a hug, his snout aligned with her nose, her air passing into him, but that was before she'd started having nightmares and needed a more reliable animal, one who wouldn't abandon her in the dark by falling out of bed.

After three weeks of Nora having to get up in the middle of the night to pacify Julia, Joseph sprang out of bed one Sunday afternoon, whistling, looking chipper.

He summoned both his daughters, having no idea which of the two was responsible. "I know a trick," he told them. "If either of yous disturb my sleep once more, I'll boot you both from here to Kingdom Come."

"I'm ashamed of myself," said Johanne, and curtsied.

"And you?" Joseph asked Julia.

"Yeah, what she said," said Julia, and curtsied.

"Lot of good that does me," he said, "when a working man needs his sleep."

❖

At her grandmother's apartment, Johanne had to sleep on the floor. Because of her bad back, there was no way her grandmother was about to give up her bed for anybody. And hadn't she warned Nora not to marry her Joseph? That he was a bad apple? Hadn't she foretold that Nora would try to leave him one day because he was never going to grow up?

"I know a trick," Johanne told Julia, imitating her father.

Before lights out, Johanne told Julia that she knew how to fly. She knew how to rise to the ceiling and guide herself with her fingertips grazing the bumpy surface.

They took turns tickling each other's backs, Johanne counting with each trace the times her sister had been brave, the times she herself had been nothing but a snivelling little sissy.

"First off you stand beside the wishing well. Want me to teach you my trick?" she asked when she got past twenty. But Julia had already dozed off, Cornelius snug behind her neck.

Johanne thought back to the day she planted marigolds in the plastic wishing well on the front lawn, the day her father told her what happens when you get older, how you get saddled with a whack of responsibilities. He stepped on the spade, shoved it into the mound of topsoil, scooped up the earth and tossed it into the well. "That's what happens," he said, as she flattened the earth with her hands. "You get buried alive."

The telephone rang. Julia reached out of her sleep to answer it. When she didn't speak, just yawned, Johanne pulled herself up to share the cradle of the phone with her.

"Tell your mother to come home," Joseph said. "Right this minute."

Julia, playing go-between, relayed her parents' messages to one another. Johanne, who had no role to play, listened to each sentence and then concentrated on the echo.

"Tell your father to go to Hell," Nora said.

"Tell her I'm coming to get her," Joseph threatened.

"He'd better not if he knows what's good for him."

"Tell her she'd better watch her back. I'll hire someone to break her legs."

"Hang up," Nora said.

"I know where you kids go to school. Tell her that."

"Hang up!" she shouted.

Johanne, wide-eyed, looked from her sister to her mother, wishing one of them would move. Nora pressed the button and cut Joseph off mid-threat, listened for a few seconds to the flat safe sound of the dial tone, and recommended the girls get back to sleep.

Johanne tiptoed over to the peephole on the front door, ran her fingers along the chain lock. Judging by the flimsy look of the thing, she figured they all had about fifteen minutes to live, all except her father's mother snoring behind her bedroom door. She stood the best chance of survival since one of the things Joseph Hamilton believed in was having respect for your elders.

"He's gonna get us," Johanne kept saying, "I *know* he's gonna get us."

"Oh, honey, your father's all talk," Nora said dismissively. "Now come back to bed. Morning comes early."

❖

Johanne and Julia had been staying with their grandmother since New Year's Eve, the night Nora had made what she called her *last* resolution. It was not until January 31 that Johanne worked up the nerve to put Julia's plan into action, peering from behind the snowbanks at home, her on one side, Julia on the other. The Buick, not in the laneway, meant their father was not home. He thought people who walked to the corner store, or even the bus stop, must have a few screws loose. He was probably at the corner store, cleaning out the Swanson TV Dinner supply.

Johanne jumped in the middle of a slush puddle, greybrown ice and water splattering on all sides. Some landed on her sister's snowsuit. Julia simply wiped it off and headed for the door. She skipped down the laneway like it was the Yellow Brick Road, singing, "We're off to see the Bugger."

The front door, as Johanne suspected, was locked. The window their mother had smashed was covered with sheet metal from their father's company. Julia slid the livingroom window open and Johanne followed her inside. She replaced the sign in the window and straightened the curtains.

The clock struck the hour above the loveseat where Nora curled up to read romance novels like *Love In The Darkness, The Secret Side Of Passion, The House Of Desire*. Everything was dead still, but had the look, Johanne thought, of things about to jump to life. Nora's figurines with the white ballgowns seemed on the verge of twirling; the family photographs seemed ready to topple forward; the front door seemed about to blow open and an icy mist come tumbling along the floor. When next she looked, she was sure to see her father standing with a knife in his hand.

The house was a pig sty, as though Joseph wasn't old enough to clean up for himself. But nothing was burning and nothing seemed broken. Her sister left sodden footprints in the blue shag. Johanne stepped inside them so as not to make more. On Johanne's way down the hall, after only eight or nine steps, there remained no wetness to step into, no form to follow. Julia's boots had dried off and she was standing in front of Joseph's bureau, sifting through a cigar box, tinkling cuff links and tie pins.

"We're gonna get caught. Let's go," Johanne said.

Julia slipped her father's big ring with her own initial on to her index finger, raising her fist to the Heavens like the mighty Hercules. Joseph's backscratcher hung on a hook over the night table. A long stem, a wooden hand, short, perfect fingernails. Julia rooted around in the litterbasket with it, retrieved a crumpled snowball of paper and batted it against the wall.

At the moment the paper hit the wall, the front door opened. "Sit," she heard her father say and immediately she lowered herself onto a corner of the bed.

"Time to go," Julia said calmly, throwing off the ring, tossing the backscratcher over Johanne's lap.

"Who's there?"

They didn't answer. Julia filed out of the room, down the hall, with Johanne, like a wagon, in tow.

"What do you want and make it snappy?" said Joseph when Julia stood in front of him with her hands on her hips. "I'm all ears." A black dog was sitting on the plastic runner. Johanne couldn't help but notice the white froth dripping from the edges of its muzzle. It was a big dog with fur taut as skin on a starving person and soon it was choking from the effort to pry itself loose. Her father yanked on the leash.

"Mom sent me to get money," Julia lied.

"Just in time to say hello to my friend here," Joseph said proudly.

He bent down on one knee to unhook the leash from the growling dog's collar and remove the muzzle. Just before the girls tore out and slammed the back door, Johanne distinctly heard their father command, "Sick." The dog's claws were clicking frantically along the plastic runner.

❖

Mr. Wilson stormed outside with his son's goalie gloves and net. He threw the net over the dog, whose snout and throat had already been wrapped tightly with Julia's long candycane toque, and he instructed both girls to wait in his house. "Alice has called in the troops," he added when they just stood there, looking on.

Not fifteen minutes passed before Nora pulled up to the house in a Blue Line Taxi.

"Joseph's not to be reasoned with," Mr. Wilson told Nora. "He says you're not leaving him. He'll keep everything. Everything from the kids' beds to their shoelaces until you come back. If you don't come back, he's going to — "

"No more, Bob, not another word."

Nora's face was as still as the house her daughters had just come from, the house before Joseph entered with the dog. Her face had a calm, Johanne judged, that was just too calm, a calm that could get everybody killed. Didn't her mother care about living, Johanne wondered. Why wasn't she afraid? Johanne would have to be worried enough for everybody.

Nora asked to use the telephone, vowing as she dialled that the first thing she was going to do when they reached Vancouver was learn how to drive.

Johanne's sister was sitting in a wingback chair, under the protective glow of a pole lamp. Her bitten hand was bandaged with white gauze and black hockey tape, all the Wilsons could find. She was leafing through the *TV Guide* as though in moments from now she'd be settling down to *Lassie* or *Bewitched* or *I Dream of Jeannie* instead of being given rabies shots at the Emergency, all those long needles digging into her navel.

Johanne promptly expressed her wish to go along.

"What for?" her mother asked.

"For company."

"Stay here. Nothing happened to *you*," she said.

Johanne waited out the few more minutes for her mother and her sister to pile into Mr. Wilson's car, using the time to gather the courage necessary to march over and confront her father, or at least scrape the hoar frost off a window and spy on him up close. She rocked from one foot to the other, the blood she had witnessed on her sister's body, and in the sludge and snow, somehow finding its way to her cheeks, somehow taking over her usually pale face.

Finally they were gone and Johanne snuck out while Alice prepared supper. Johanne grew calmer as she began her short walk. Cool, weightless flakes of snow fell on her hair, her eyelashes, between her collar and neck. In front of her family's house, behind a snowbank, she stood with palms up, hoping that what melted there on her woollen mittens would accumulate, solidify, protect her. She pictured hot orange sparks from her father's blowtorch, rebounding like hard glass beads, disappearing afterward in the air.

❖

The front door creaked open. Out came Joseph who threw Nora's soup tureen and ladle; both landed at the base of the wishing well. The marigolds were crisp and frozen and shrivelled.

In less than a moment, Johanne had flown out of herself, above the house, and hovered there in a horizontal position. She floated as the snow whirled round and round her; a wind, light as her own breath, whispered something soothing into her ears.

When she searched below, from some fifty yards above, she was practically certain she could discern the form of a disoriented black dog buffeting the snowbanks along Shillington Avenue. The body of her father looked minuscule also and busy as the snowflakes around her, as busy as a blizzard of orange sparks. Hard as she tried though, she could not make out what he was doing. Her snow-encrusted eyes strained to see more clearly, but when she raised her hand to clear her lashes, she plummeted back to herself on the ground.

Her father, she could see now, was pasting other signs in the window, so that it was practically covered. KEEP OFF THE GRASS. FOR SALE. NO SOLICITING. NO PARKING. EMPLOYEES ONLY. ROOM FOR RENT. KEEP OUT. NO TRESPASSING. NO SMOKING. BEWARE OF DOG. In front of her feet, chunks of ice had been stabbed by a shovel or the plow, and piled like their yearly Christmas presents. When Johanne reached down to gather up a few she realized she had to go to the bathroom.

She dropped the ice chunks, keeping one the perfect size and weight. She moved closer and heaved it at the window. The ice resounded against the glass, but didn't break it. She turned and ran away, secreting herself by the Wilsons' side door to crouch and allow the urine to slide warmly down her leggings.

"Where's your sister?" she could hear her father calling. "Where's your mother?" There was nothing after that; he'd slipped back inside.

Johanne started to make snowballs, clapping her hands together, one over the other until she figured she had formed a wall of fifty. She envisioned each of the signs in her livingroom window covered with white.

Her plan was to move closer, little by little, and cover the whole rectangle of window and the little sliding windows along the bottom. So what if her father was inside sharpening knives. She wouldn't stop throwing snowballs until the whole house looked like a giant igloo. She wouldn't stop until her sister and her mother came home. By then her arms would be *made* of muscles, bulging, rigid muscles from all her hard work. Muscles that she could flex proudly as she boasted to her sister she no longer knew the first thing about flying.

Hugging The Urn

STEP INTO MY PARLOUR SAID THAT LADY, WHO NEVER WENT anywhere unless where she went was with a flyswatter. It was winter and there were no flies in the house; there was just Daddy, present for ten minutes, present for two Swats on what I'd heard mothers in our neighbourhood refer to as his *Cute Little Caboose*. Daddy told That Lady a secret and this was when he got his second swat.

I must have been ten when he dropped us at That Lady's house. It was mid-morning, right after Ramone had styled Daddy's hair and given me and Willie pixies. With the pixie I looked like a boy, my brother like the village idiot, and That Lady couldn't help herself from saying so. I thought she was one to talk with that Chestnut spume of roots on both sides of her part which might easily have been mistaken, from afar, for the caterpillars which slithered up the bark of our Poplars. I thought if I had to sit there anyway, I might as well make the best of it and render her unmistakable likeness on a sheet of stark White paper. Of all my artistic endeavours, rendering true to life portraits was my specialty.

"You be good and listen to This Lady in the pedal pushers and the clodhoppers. Don't give her a hard time, her mind is on other matters," he said on his way out, pointing to her, winking. He blew two kisses at us, and I snatched them out of the air before she could snag them for herself.

Like two Angels we sat on her chesterfield, holding hands, watching her watch him through the window, watching her hug the flyswatter, the way I'd seen people hug on *The Edge Of Night*. She started to waltz with her eyes closed, humming, "There's something about an Aqua Velva man."

They didn't call me Boldilocks for nothing so I told That Lady we'd rather be in Reform School than have to sit there and listen to Her try to carry a tune. I told her flies hibernated and that she ought to consider doing the same. I advised her to remember the facts of life: there was no Santa Claus and babies came out your bum. I told her Daddy was Some Handsome Cutie Pie and that so many ladies seemed to think so. How did she like them apples?

For a full sixty seconds she stared me down. Where did I come from, she wanted to know, as though I were from outer space. She then ordered Willie and me into the kitchen for lunch. Between the four burners on the stove she slapped the flyswatter down. She whipped up Kraft Dinner and fried Spam sandwiches. I informed her, shoving the plates and bowls back across the formica table, that Willie was allergic to dairy and that I had a thing about people's dirty hands coming into contact with my food.

"You, Lady Jane and You, Mister Man will eat what's put in front of you. Or you'll both get a lickin'," she said, but she had rearranged the dishes before shoving them back so that Willie now had two sandwiches, and me two bowls of noodles.

"Have you ever seen an allergic reaction?" I sassed her, ready to describe one.

"Yes, I have," she said, "and it would serve the whole bunch of you right."

❖

There was the time Daddy offered Nancy and Janet's mother a ride to work one morning just because it was drizzling; I faked having the Asian Flu.

There was the time Daddy sent me to the library to look up the recipe for Mint Juleps, so he and Mrs. Baker, the mother of my deaf friend Elise, could sit in the backyard in her parked motor boat to drink them, him in his bathing suit, her in a bra and panties set she'd dyed Magenta.

"Just like a bikini," I signed to her, letter by letter, "I bet nobody knows the difference."

There was the time Daddy wanted to name our new dog after an old flame, Trudy; I convinced Mommy the dog was being named after Gertrude Stein, whom I'd just heard of from the Guidance Counsellor. A dog is a dog is a dog, I told Mommy, trusting the repetition would incline her to believe me.

And then, the time I caught him kissing Mommy's best friend and bingo buddy, Mrs. Jarvis.

Both families, minus Mr. Jarvis, were in the backyard roasting wienies and marshmallows over a bonfire. Somehow, like in all quaint love stories, everybody except the Happy Couple conveniently disappeared. Mommy excused herself to put together a tray of fixings for the wienies and I was sent to the Jarvis' to fetch a bottle of her famous chutney. I remember it being Umber or Burnt Sienna colour, with thick chunks of onion packed inside the mason jar; the same hue and texture I had been after for the rolling hills in my latest water colour landscape.

The jar slipped out of my hand and crashed to the floor. When I went to the window to call out for a dustpan, that's when I saw it. Daddy's face planted on hers, moving ever so slightly, one hand at the back of her neck, one passing over her bare, bony knee caps.

It was the first time in years I had given a thought to That Lady, and here was another one Begging to be put in her place. These women had what Mommy called the nerve of Dick Tracy, Audacity in Spades, which allowed them to flaunt things right under her nose.

I remembered that when Daddy had come back to get us, he knocked his head on an Ochre strip of fly paper That Lady had hanging from the ceiling in her front entrance. "Jesus H!," he said. But it had no flies on it which, I told her, was a good thing because Daddy was very particular about his Coiffure. Daddy tossed her a pack of Sweet Tarts, thanked her.

"Any time," she told him. I was confident she didn't mean it.

We said goodbye and we were off in his Scarlet convertible. We swung round to Consumers' to pick up Mommy who primly settled herself in the front seat and fastened her kerchief over her head. Just as rehearsed between us, Willie and I told Mommy what a fine babysitter That Lady had been and what an old crone too.

"She was a fine babysitter, Mommy," said Willie.

"Jolly good sport!" I added.

❖

Mommy always said that we, as the Caretaking Sex, had to allow men their dalliances. Mommy stood before her soaps every week day and ironed at least one waffle-like triangle on to another of Daddy's good cotton shirts. I blew Caramel paint onto paper through straws, trying to capture the Effect.

We had to let them get their hands dirty is the way she put it. There was no harm in finger painting, the way I did it, to be sure, as long as it was just an experiment and, as long as it didn't make too much of a mess. As long as it wasn't held up, she said, and taken for the Real Enchilada.

Even though she travelled like a nomad every night, going from room to room with her fold-up cot, it wasn't until I was a teenager that I realized she had never put that much stock in her own words. She had only ever really turned a blind eye to Married Women.

When Daddy took up with Gail across the street, Gail, the Strumpet Divorcée, Mommy decided it was high time the line was drawn. She packed up all of Daddy's clothes, except his underwear and hair products which she said he wouldn't be needing, and soon Gail's front lawn was littered with Samsonite luggage.

For good measure, Mommy marooned Trudy, our dog. She tied her, all weepy and forlorn, to a bald birch tree at the community park. A map attached to its collar directed any finder to the house of Mrs. Gertrude Schuster and a tiny *nota bene* in the corner confirmed that the dog's food of choice was Dr. Ballard's, spiced up with a dash or two of Worchesterchire Sauce.

According to Mommy, it was a fortuitous good thing Somebody around there knew Something about Commitment.

❖

There was to be no talk of divorce; she'd never, being the good Catholic that she was, grant him one. And there was to be no talk of our father's Baby Girl, Gail.

"I don't mean you, Sylvia," Mommy would say to me.

"I don't mean your sister," she'd say to Willie.

"I mean Her," she'd say, which gave Mommy the needed excuse to peep out the window to watch the Comings and Goings of Judas Priest and his Magdalene. Give us a running commentary.

> They're getting out of the car.
> He opened her door for Her.
> They're holding hands.
> Aren't they just a Pair of Love Birds?
> Isn't he ever just so solicitous?
> He can't find the house keys.
> He's rummaging through his pockets.
> Oh just Like Her to keep one under the Welcome Mat.

For a whole year Mommy kept this up. Daddy wouldn't get his divorce, not that he ever asked for one, and my paintings were hanging in the Gallery — that was good enough for her. The Gallery had previously been the Master Bedroom, converted for revenge to show off my Art and purge the room of Daddy's infectious germs. *Nice*, Mommy would say of my collages of female cut-out dolls. *Bold*, she would say of my splatterings of Pervenche et Saumon. *Extraordinary!* she would pipe up when Daddy was hanging around, trying to win back her affection.

When Daddy ceased and desisted, for he got no encouragement from Scorned and Wounded Mommy, the Gallery, with the exception of the walls, was given over to two brothers, twins, in Medical School, who made up for their cheap room and board by putting Mommy's blood and urine under the microscope for free. For free, they told her one day that she'd better pay a visit to her family physician. Something they had discovered didn't look exactly normal.

❖

In spite of a hack job mastectomy and a fair-to-middling prognosis, Mommy died when I was twenty, full of morphine and in agony on her fold-up cot. It had been first set up in the kitchen where it would be convenient for Willie and me to make, fetch and feed her ice cubes. But then Daddy got wind of a decline in her spirits. He moved back in and moved Mommy back to the Gallery, which he referred to by its former name, The Love Nest. She was still alert enough to protest, but she did not.

To pass the hours, the two occasionally extemporized on the effect their relationship over the years had had on my Art Work.

"She's like her Father. Doesn't want to grow up and simmer down," Mommy was oft to repeat.

"You mean like her Mother," Daddy would retort, wiping her brow with a cool cloth. "Thinks she's got the answer for everything."

In any event, both agreed my having an eye for detail and for colour would make me a competent decorator and eventually, if my wisecracking mouth didn't get me into trouble, land me a good man who would buy me a house to play in. I was not likely, the two thought, to suddenly veer off into the paying professions of Secretary, Teacher or Nurse, but neither was I expected to wind up an Old Maid.

This reference to the Kind of woman I wouldn't wind up as

inevitably introduced tide-like allusions to the women and Kind of women Daddy kept up appearances for, the Kind of women with whom he had kept company behind Mommy's back.

The day of her death, they carried on as if Willie and me weren't there. Listening in on their secrets fooled us into thinking we could keep Mommy with us forever, into thinking Mommy and Daddy would pick up right where they'd left off.

"Mrs. Schuster," he admitted.

"I knew it!" she said.

"Mrs. Avon."

"In Winter of '71. And don't forget Darryl's wife, nor that brazen Pat Jarvis."

He stared at her, reddened and benumbed.

"No good to lie," she said. "Everybody knew."

"Rest assured, Mother," he said, squeezing her two hands more tightly. "I never gave my heart to Another."

"I know, I know," she said. "But likely you'll replace me with Another the instant I'm gone. I do believe, moreover, that your hair is just slightly out of place."

I could visualize the exclamation point at the end of the sentence and her arched eyebrows accusing, though Daddy's six-foot frame blocked her from view. Having slipped in the last shrewd and inscrutable word, she expired, probably with a smile on her face, with Daddy standing over her — shocked, dismayed, horrified — trying to shake her back alive.

❖

"The Irony," said Daddy, emerging all at once from his stupor, "is of course that the female areola was my weakness. All sizes, all shapes. Every blasted colour from Pink to Tan."

HUGGING THE URN

It was a hot, sticky evening, around eight o'clock. Willie, Daddy and me were alone in the backyard, watching the Plum sun set, quarter by quarter. Mommy's urn, that looked in one way like Tarnished Silver but in another like Gleaming Mica, stood on the patio table, dwarfed by the big umbrella. Gone the way of her body, and her own two breasts, was the powder of her ashes, sprinkled in the garden like fertilizer.

The funeral, five days prior, had run at a good clip. Plenty of family had attended, but no friends because Mommy had, long before that, stopped having them. Every single one of Daddy's cohorts paid their respects, at least, I surmised, the ones that lived in town. All of them were escorted by their Cuckolded Husbands, which was dignified and proper and Daddy only cursorily thanked them for coming, which was likewise dignified and proper.

Gail, being unmarried, did not show.

And I was thankful for it, until in strode That Lady. There was no mistaking Her; she had the same Platinum hair and the same Chestnut roots. Unmistakably too, she was pregnant, and yet, from what I could see, manless.

She made her way directly for Daddy, whispered something in his ear, or maybe she was nibbling on his ear lobe I thought, then she moved to Mommy's body in the coffin. Genuflected beside her in solemn-looking prayer. It hit me! I should approach That Lady and go, "Catch any flies lately?" Smack her upside the head.

As life, crazy with all its ironies, would have it, that very thing, a fly, began to whirl around, stopping every now and again to skitter across Mommy's Ivory blouse. Daddy spotted it at once and started a commotion by trying to shoo it away.

Willie, equally frantic, searched around the parlour for something with which to swat the fly, his eyes finally coming to rest on the Guest Book, signed, Dick Tracyly, I had already remarked, by all the women present. Before he could flatten the fly, That Lady side-swiped it in her palm, shook her fist a couple of times to daze it and then strode to the front and ceremoniously let it out of doors. Daddy loped over and kissed her cheek in front of Everybody. Ran his hand over her belly.

In the backyard, on the night we scattered the ashes, I expressed to Daddy my relief, if you could call it that, at being told by some aunt that the child That Lady carried did not belong to Him. At this, he broke into laughter, then his expression went plain.

"For God's sake, Sylvia, That Lady is your sister!" he said. "Well, your half-sister, from my first marriage. Poor thing, got caught in the middle when I had to leave her mother for your mother."

I persisted. For his information, That Lady had fed Willie dairy, knowing he was allergic. She might have killed us both, I told him, if Daddy hadn't finally come back to get us That Day. How dare he become involved with someone who drooled over him the way she did. Because of Mommy everything took on such large proportions but because of Him and his Baby Girl's Hotsy Totsy Hooters, I said, I had never been able to capture the stillness of moments in my painting. "Is there ice in your veins, you asshole?" I said. And, what first marriage was he talking about, pray tell?

"She's my daughter," he repeated. "I'm not asking you to be friends."

"Give your head a shake, if you think you can start up with her and at the same time have one moment's peace."

Huge cotton batting clouds seemed so close to my head as to keep me from fidgeting. He shook me a couple of times, repeated her name and that she was his daughter, his daughter, his daughter. Not an ex-girlfriend. He shared a brief history, and then the bitter circumstances under which he had been forced to leave. In short, falling in love was the last thing you were supposed to do in a love affair, and keeping yourself from getting caught, that was the first. Tammy, he called her, though a sweet kid, had always had a weakness for luring men into her life so she could break their hearts. This was the one thing he and Tammy had in common.

"I'm glad for her she found someone decent. She did a sweet thing today. For me. For Mother," he said.

A tear welled up in each of his eyes; both tears stretched over his plain, tired face. He reached for the urn and sat it in his lap. His back hunched protectively over absent Mommy, whom he clutched with fierce, more determined hands.

I hurried into the house to grab a sketchpad and Charcoal pencil to capture the outline, the curvature, but only my paints and brushes seemed to be on hand. These wouldn't do and so I settled on Mommy's camera, loaded it quickly with film, pressed a flash cube on top.

I wanted to stare through the lens at what would become *the* Photograph of my parents together. Eventually, to hold that Photograph in my hand. And I wanted people to respect the Photograph as Proof of what I saw, but also, what was Manifestly There.

As with my Art, in the grips of the same propelling sense of animation, I was already thinking up a title. *Night Hugging Daddy And Daddy Hugging The Urn.* In the bottommost right hand corner, with a thick Black scrawl, I had already signed my name. Already, I had framed the Photograph ornately, and hung it in the Love Nest above Mommy's fold-away cot.

The Simple Life

IT'S MIDNIGHT, STILL RAINING AND GORDON RACICOT'S FLIGHT has been delayed.

He has just finished saying to Emmeline, the half-naked stranger behind him in the bed, that the old bugger between his legs has seen livelier days. Whether or not she believes him is another story, but her arms encircle his waist, that hottest part of him, the way the equator encircles the globe. Her arms are what hold his hemispheres together, the part of him that wants to leave, the part with nowhere to go.

"Hell of a downpour," he says, getting up, positioning himself in front of the hotel's big window. "Doesn't seem to be letting up whatsoever."

"I love a storm," says Emmeline. She is seated against the headboard, a pillow between her legs. "I'd rather go to a storm than go to a movie. How about you?"

"That would depend on who's directing, now wouldn't it?"

Outside, lightning flashes through the clouds, giving the sky the look of an X-ray. It's so dark out there Gordon can't see the storm anymore. He can only hear it, relieving itself against the pavement and the glass with a steady pulse of gushes. Coming down in buckets, his Aunt Livvy would say if she were here. But of course she's not here, she's dead, and the rain is what's keeping Gordon from her funeral.

Emmeline is smiling at him. Not a solicitous and helpful smile like the one when he first caught her eye, but a cocky, arrogant smile, full of gleaming white teeth, every one of them saying she knows how irresistible she is. It's the first time he has looked at her directly since spotting her at the airport and she is really quite pretty. Pretty with the large, open features of young people who take care of themselves — who *do not* smoke, who *do* avoid the sun, who *do* manage to get enough sleep. Her hair is that dirty blonde colour, all neatly pinned up. He has an urge to approach her and remove the bobby pins, make a game of it, discover if her hair falls to shoulder length the way the hair of every woman should.

Emmeline pats the mattress, playfully spanks it. Gordon remembers with disdain that women can tempt you into compromising situations if you're not on your guard, make you feel, after it's over, that you're the one who initiated things, with your base and vile animalism. Women can stand there with their sickly bodies run to fat in their filthy godforsaken homes and ask *you* what is wrong with *your* little boy parts. Make you spend the rest of your life feeling like two cents.

A familiar anxiety flushes his face, moves over the trunk of his body. He's wearing the Calvin Klein undershirt and underwear his wife bought him for Valentine's Day. Grey, form-fitting, though not too snug; satisfaction guaranteed or your money cheerfully refunded. Emmeline's eyes make him feel like a patient in his doctor's office.

"I'm happily married," he offers and begins to inspect the

heavy-duty lining of the curtains. "Twenty-seven years. To the same woman. Her name is Irene. She's bright, funny, feisty, sensitive, generous, imaginative, talented. You know last month she made this — " He lets the sentence trail off. "And she has the patience of a saint."

She'd have to. Gordon thinks up Emmeline's rebuttal for her before she can. It's what he would say if he were in her shoes. After a few seconds it's clear the girl's willing to go on listening without making snide remarks, so, for a temptress she's very polite, he thinks. He likes a good listener.

Earlier, in the airport terminal, he had thought her pushy, no different from all the rest. She had looped her arm around his and guided him to a dark and cozy corner, away from the other passengers who were munching on sandwiches and drinking coffee — Air Canada refreshments in recompense for the inconvenience of inclement weather. All he could distinguish outside was the Boeing 747 and beyond that, the lights on the runway. In his peripheral vision he could make out the unbelievably large, indiscriminating eyes of the girl.

"No passengers, no destination. A plane," he'd said flatly to her, "is unremarkable except in flight."

"Obviously you've never done it in a cockpit," had been her answer.

And then, when the delay slid into a confirmed cancellation, he found himself in a cab, the girl leaning against his shoulder, her hand poised on one of his knees. Through the rearview mirror, the driver kept locking eyes with Gordon, either in judgement or envy. The car moved slowly. Beads of water blurred the colours and the lights of the downtown core, as well as Gordon's sense of direction. The guy could have been driving around in circles, tripling or quadrupling his entitled fare; Gordon was in no hurry. If he had had to sit in the cab all night, driving around, it would hardly have killed him. Because he was tanked on Glenfiddich, it was easy to pretend the car sailing through the streets of Ottawa was a gondola sailing through the canals of Venice. He had been in no hurry to get himself to this hotel room.

"As we're sitting there, you know, back at the airport," Emmeline says, "I'm watching you, the way you're eyeing the stewardess with the coffee tray. Here's a flirt. I'm watching you and I'm thinking yes here's a flirt AND a distinguished looking man. I'm thinking healthy specimen this one and I'm thinking, ripe for a little adventure. This is gonna be a walk in the park."

"I've never done this sort of thing before," he claims. He claims to be a man who doesn't go around doing this sort of thing.

"Compared to you, I may be just a kid, but I wasn't born yesterday."

He tries to steady his warbling voice by swallowing, warning her again he might not be able to deliver. He has just gotten over a bout of strep throat and he mightn't be able to, you know, *deliver*. "Then you'll want to kick yourself for having thought this up."

She laughs, undeterred by the challenge, keener even. "You have a mouth, you have fingers. So what say I bet you a tour of my body you can't stand way over there all night," says Emmeline, now kneeling, offering up as bait her proud, puffy nipples, the black lace of her panties.

"It's a bet you would lose," he tries to assure her. But suddenly he is closer to her, further from the window, sitting at the desk. He picks up a pen and starts to doodle on the hotel stationery.

"I'm going to run you a hot bath. You'll see I'm deadly with a bar of soap."

Gordon knows he could dress and slip down into the bar or an alcove of the lobby while the girl is in the bathroom. He's not aroused, why should he stay? He doesn't want to hurt

Irene. He doesn't want to hurt the girl. It's never been his intention to hurt anyone, in fact it's always *him* that gets hurt in the end.

With every ounce of his energy and fortitude, he has always tried to make them sense his ambivalence, tried to will them into seeing his ordinariness, into wanting him for something less. Ask him on any given day and he will tell you all he wants is the simple life — food, shelter, somebody to love him, coasting under clear blue skies for the rest of his days. It's in his bones, in his blood. And for the whole of his life he has been faithfully wed to the conviction that it's not asking for too much.

"Coming?" Emmeline calls from the bathroom.

He picks up the phone and orders a bottle of Chianti Ruffino and a platter of crudités from Room Service. Before he can stop himself he is on the line with the front desk, ordering a pornographic movie.

❖

Gordon, reclined in the tub, is admiring the opalescent bubbles all over his chest, the sheen of near pinks and blues. The water is hot, Emmeline's hands, so warm and soothing. Moments ago, he tried to call the shots by demanding she avert her eyes as he undressed, then by talking football scores — CFL, NFL, even the American college teams — as she knelt there, outside the water, sipping her wine. But she tired of it, told him they would take things so slow he would think nothing was happening and now this, like so many events in his life, seems out of his hands.

"So, you're headed to a funeral? Whose, if you don't mind

my asking?" asks Emmeline, her fingers sculpting little peaks out of bubbles and his chest hairs.

"My aunt Livvy."

"Were you close?"

"Not in recent years."

He draws the entire contents of his wine glass in one go and Emmeline pours him more. With his eyes shut against the muted light, the pores of his skin open to Emmeline's soft hands, he can see his aunt in perfect detail. A short woman with short purplish auburn hair standing on her skinny flamingo legs, giving some boyfriend a pedicure. She's rattling on about being a faithful churchgoer, a person who feeds the stray cats in her neighbourhood, a person who does her damndest to make sure nobody goes alone or presentless on Christmas. She will get around sooner or later to boasting she has a ragbag of attentive men and a string of conquests behind her as long as the Macy's Parade, which she attends without fail every year.

"What'd she die of?"

"Guilt, if there's a God, and something far less excruciating if there isn't," Gordon says. He goes on to say that she was a hypochondriac whose sense of drama mixed with just enough immodesty could solicit anyone, a complete stranger even, to smell her fingertips and her bowel movements stagnating in the toilet, let her know if they were metallic-like. The last he'd heard she'd diagnosed herself with cystic fibrosis.

"This is how she talked. 'Gordie, oh Gordie, I'm having a spell. Gordie, oh Gordie, it's so drafty in here. Come here. Sit down beside me, Gordie, and hold my hand won't you, Gordie? Why don't you be a good boy? Gordie, oh Gordie.' It's a wonder she never thought to contract something from her poor living conditions," Gordon adds.

Aunt Livvy had a way of making her house look squeaky clean, even if it wasn't. To disinfect it, she doused the plastic on the furniture and lampshades with vinegar, thick as the fog of her cheap perfume. Summers, in the old days when Gordon and Phil had to stay with her, she'd put them to work and once the job was done, pay them each a quarter to scram, get, make themselves scarce. One of her boyfriends was on his way over and she still had some articles to hide that were none of anybody's business but family.

Ralph the Rover, or Timothy Thingamajig the Third or Curious George McGowan, as Gordon and Phil referred to them, were not about to open any closet door to discover all her posters of Marilyn Monroe, or peep under the skirt of her bed where she stockpiled all the dirty clothes until the calendar indicated *Laundromat Adventure Weekend* with a big black asterisk. Only a real insider, like her nephews, would be privy to what treasures got crammed and grew mouldy under the cushions and in the cracks of the chesterfield. Bologna sandwiches, for one, slapped together with spotted, turquoise bread.

With their measly quarters, Gordon and Philip would each buy a bruisey blue jawbreaker and a bottle of cream soda. They'd ride their bikes home to Aunt Livvy's as fast as their legs could pedal and station themselves by the back screen door, or under the deck, itching to hear some scandalous thing they'd be able to use against her the next time their father got it in his mind to leave them in her care.

Gordon remembers asking Phil what all the bozos saw in her, remembers being told the attraction was Livvy's jugs which, without exaggerating, were the size of watermelons, every sane man's fantasy. Livvy did strut around referring to herself as a full-figured woman, like Marilyn, but Gordon couldn't believe that was it because Aunt Livvy, apart from her jugs, was offensive to look at. Philip said females all looked the same in the dark and still Gordon wasn't convinced. What sane man would *choose* to pick his way through Aunt Livvy's mess, peel off her garish underwear, those dingy elasticized underwear just thirsting for bleach? To get a peek at what? He didn't know what was supposed to be so special about jugs likes hers. You couldn't even fit them in your hands.

"I couldn't wait for the day I'd never have to lay eyes on her again."

"Well, lean back, relax, 'cause now you don't have to." Emmeline bends over the tub and kisses each of his nipples, his navel. When she is kneeling upright again she asks, "How come your wife's not going? I thought these things were supposed to be family affairs."

"Wives and funerals. Now talk like that's not very conducive," Gordon says, reaching out his right hand by way of an invitation in.

Emmeline climbs into the tub, straddles his shins and begins to massage his thighs. That part of him isn't submerged and so, until she realizes she must wet him properly, there will be friction between her skin and his hair. Fantasizing this, Gordon would have imagined the sound and the movement to be slight, almost imperceptible — she's very petite, some might even say delicate. But this rubbing of hers is so grating and so gritty. He gestures for her to stop.

"Personal talk, off limits. I see," she says and draws a horizontal line through the air, as though she were scratching this subject off a list, then she splashes him lightly. "Next you'll be telling me you have something against dirty talk, what with you being a choirboy and all. I think I know the drill."

"How many lovers have you had?" Gordon asks, smiling just enough to appear interested. "Many?"

"He asks about quantity when he can ask about quality. I'm disappointed. Usually the question is who was your last or, who was your first. I think it's a sign of maturity to want to know a person's history."

"Too much history, not enough mystery," he says, holding

his empty glass aloft, closing his eyes again. "But you can tell me. Who was your first?"

"Relax, let yourself go," says Emmeline since Gordon has begun to squirm under her touch. "Who was yours?"

Emmeline, with her feet, is causing Gordon's penis to bob in the water, poke holes through the bubbles that have become a thin and vaporous looking cloud which can't seem to stay in one place for very long at all. She slides him between her toes as she slides soap between her palms, lather emerging from every crack. The bar of soap, all slippery, splashes into the water, thuds against the enamel.

Gordon, his breathing quiet and stealthy as a sickness, looks up at the white ceiling and tries to forget who he is.

❖

"My turn," says Emmeline, guiding Gordon's head down between her legs, where the pillow once was. Emmeline and Gordon are back in bed. The girl has stripped it of sheets and blankets, so now it's just the two of them, Gordon Racicot and Emmeline, last name unknown and unasked for. Gordon feels he is suffocating, bucks, and comes up for air.

"You know something, I think I'm a little tired," he announces.

"From what? You haven't done a thing. If anybody's got a right to be tired, it's me. And I am. Sick and tired," She marches off to the bathroom again, this time slamming the door.

Gordon puts his underwear back on and makes the bed, tucking sheets in at the foot of it, leaving them loose at the head. He drapes the bedspread over a wingchair by the window, returns to fluff and prop up the pillows, climbs in and makes himself comfortable. It occurs to him to phone Irene, but it might be in bad taste. What if the girl were to overhear and go berzerk? Just four days ago, Irene had a dream with a similar plot line, a premonition, and if he can remember correctly, he was the one who wound up dead, a knife in the back.

Instead he laces his fingers together in his lap, settles back to watch the pornographic movie playing on the television. A threesome made up of a white woman sandwiched between two black men is going at it on a table in a library. The men have a lost look about them while the woman appears to be in deep concentration over where to locate the pleasure. The camera fades out and shows the woman in a bar, eyeing the two men who are dressed in suits and engaged in discussion over an important-looking document. The threesome was her fantasy. It was *her* fantasy and still she couldn't be satisfied.

Coach Boisvert, when Gordon was eleven, swore it was well nigh impossible to satisfy a woman. Boys must understand that girl parts were tucked away, mysteriously and frustratingly, inside them. It behooved him to add that sex was a game, the objective of which was to score baskets. Score points without committing a foul. What you wanted was to win, but not so badly that a ball fell all the way through and the girl had to walk around with it under her dress. That was a definite violation. One that could make you wish you'd stayed in the audience instead of swapping tall tales in the locker room and heading out onto the court with a heaping hornet's nest of hormones.

That Gordon might eventually have sex with someone who was cute and a virgin was the one thing which managed to keep him glued together during his high school years. Which was odd because the thought of anybody else having sex, even the girl he would have to have it with one day, gave him the willies. The position (for then he only knew of the one) seemed to him preposterous and humiliating. He'd walked in on his father once and there was good old dad and the ghostly white mounds of his ass pumping up and down as though to save his very soul.

Too bad sex was an act you had to perform without your clothes on. Worse was that you had to lie in that condition afterward, running down the clock, pretending the other person still possessed something you wanted and needed. Coach Boisvert said that the seemly thing to do after intercourse was to lie there and take it like a man. They, meaning the girls, liked it when you touched their hair or counted the vertebrae of their bare backs.

Pretend you want to be there, Coach had said. Once it was done, you were not to make out as if you'd rather be shooting hoops with the guys because you were going to want to get back in the game at some point. To highlight his conviction Coach Boisvert drew tantalizing pink diagrams of *vagina* and *clitoris* on the chalkboard.

Aunt Livvy, however, had gotten to Gordon first. Aunt Livvy had called Coach Boisvert's *vagina* a twat; she had called his *clitoris* a cookie. Cookie, she'd said, was the key to everything and once Gordon understood that, he'd be all set, wouldn't require anymore lessons.

He'd have liked to have been brave enough not to do as she asked. He'd have liked to never set eyes on her again, but his father kept sending him back. Insisted on it. Time and time again, no matter how much of a stink he raised. Livvy was Gordon's only aunt on his father's side, a woman whose peccadilloes he was urged to overlook since she was someone who obviously meant well. His father told him that when he and Livvy were kids, Livvy took a fire poker through the calf, trying to prevent his being beaten, that's why one of her legs was so skinny. The only say Gordon and Philip were about to have in any family matter was whether to mow the lawn first or wash the car.

So, at a time when Gordon had been in a hurry to "do the deed" so very badly, go all the way, Aunt Livvy was hysterical to have him done with it. She threw her hands in the air much the same way as the naked woman doing it on television. "Hustle," she'd say. "What are you waiting for? The right one?" According to her, there was no right one. Even when you were sure you'd found that right one, it all amounted to no more than a hill of beans in the end. "Love!" she'd exclaim and almost spit at it. "Just grow up."

Aunt Livvy swore she would fire off a few letters of entreaty to "Mademoiselle Labelle" from the notorious Agency, or actually dawdle on through the red light district with him until he picked one for himself and solved the big mystery. Did he want to be a virgin forever, a punk with pimples, blackheads and a yearbook full of unattainable beauties he could only hope to reach by pulling his pin over their pictures?

"Come on, Gordie, I'll help you."

That she didn't like little boys was the only explanation she would offer for her gusto in this regard. Little boys, with all their fumbling and those Romper Room antics. "Cripes almighty! Why can't you boys be trailblazers for a refreshing change? Why does it always have to be me to take you by the hand and teach the way? I swear, if your little thingy could speak English, you still wouldn't know what to do with it."

Years after he'd been married, when Gordon finally booked an appointment with his doctor, the doctor chastened him for not mentioning his little problem sooner. These problems could be taken care of in a jiffy. Over Gordon's twenty-seven-year marriage to Irene, Gordon had been in the office countless times, for one sorry ailment after another — bowel spasms, panic attacks, chest pains, ulcers and hives, and Gordon had never mentioned this other.

The doctor gave Gordon simple exercises to try, exercises that were sure to turn him into a paragon of virility. Gordon agreed to a month, then wrote himself off as a failure. To Irene, it didn't matter one whit and never had, as long as he still loved her. "I didn't marry you for that part of it," she continues to insist. "You're still the man I married."

"Hey, Emmeline, what's taking you?" Then glimpsing the television, he calls, "Hey, Cookie!"

"You can go straight to hell. Take your time. Have yourself a little snooze along the way," she answers.

Emmeline, out of the bathroom a few seconds later, has obviously been crying. Her cheeks are sodden and puffy looking, like her nipples. She steps into a pair of navy blue pumps. Her blouse is buttoned up and she's searching the room for her skirt. After she finds it and puts it on, she removes her right shoe and hurls it, with fair warning, at Gordon's head. He catches it and lets it fall to the floor. Hail stones outside simultaneously pelt the window, but she doesn't notice, is removing the other shoe and taking aim.

"Next time, don't start something you can't finish," she says, pointing the shoe the way a parent might wag an index finger.

"Me?"

"Yeah you."

"Did I or did I not warn you this would happen? This is what always happens. You picked the wrong guy, that's all. A girl like you, you could have anybody you want. That airport was full of young studs with the stamina for six times a night. Why didn't you pick one of them?"

She is crying again, with as much ease as she earlier removed her clothes, and made the offer of her body. "What's wrong with me? Why don't you like me?" She's imploring, begging now for them to try again. She wants to know if it's because of her body, or her face, or something else she hasn't tried her best to make appealing. Her spirits seem to soar when it occurs to her Gordon might not find her so bad with the lights off.

"No."

With the heel of the shoe, she is suddenly beating herself, the top of her head, her nose, chin, clavicle bone, her sternum. He springs up to take hold of her wrists. They scuffle, lose their balance and fall back into bed.

In the dark, he lets down her hair and removes her blouse. Up and down the column of her spine, he runs his fingertips, his tongue, pressing hard to make sure she can feel him. All the while, as she sobs, he whispers that she is beautiful, so beautiful, how can she not know this? He wants to position them both in front of a mirror and point himself out. He's the one. It's him. He's so *defective* and he's sorry. Nothing would make him feel better at this moment than to show her who she is, a special person some special man is going to snap right up.

"This is special," she says, cooing sleepily. "Us lying naked together."

"Yes," he whispers.

After a while, he realizes he has been talking incessantly and that his words, like a lullaby, have led her gently into sleep. Now that she's asleep, he tells her about Italy. How in this life or the next, he would like to be camped under the dome of the Sistine Chapel, making long religious love to his wife. Because he hasn't. Ever. What he's trying to do, as he explains this, is teach. Not the way he learned, but what. That life is hard enough without being distracted by people who cannot possibly save you.

Emmeline's body, in smaller dimension, follows the contours of his skin, muscles, bones — her back against his chest, her buttocks on his genitals, the backs of her legs over his thighs, knees over knees, the balls of her feet poised on his shins. She is within the circle of his arms.

Having breathed in the lilac scent of her hair and listened to rain most of the night, Gordon falls asleep close to dawn. He falls into dreams of funerals where the rain is driving down, lowering the coffins into the bowels of the earth. He falls into dreams of far-off places he has never before imagined or travelled to, Emmeline's navy blue shoe cradled in his hand.

Chocolate Rosebuds

I JUST HATED IT WHEN LADIES PATTED THEIR HAIR DOWN BEFORE they opened up their front doors. How they ran their hands over their hips to smooth their pretty dresses. I mean really, who were they trying to kid? A wrinkle on a dress didn't make the dress not a pretty one, and hair was either messy or it wasn't. One little pat wasn't gonna do them any good and sweet Jesus if the dress was creased no amount of smoothing at the last second was gonna fix it. Just open up the fucking door.

But there she was. I could see her through the little window beside the door, doing what I hated and what made me sick as a dog. There was this little shear curtain and with the hall lights on she knew damn well I could see her, she just *knew*. She could stand around looking at herself in front of a mirror for quite a few minutes, knowing somebody was standing outside waiting. What did that say?

Well as soon as she let me in, the look she gave me was out

of this world, like I wasn't worth the time she spent fussing for me, which was pretty funny when you think of it 'cause she probably went to the hairdresser and had a perm done and all for a chick my age. All for nobody. You should have seen the disappointment on her face, written all over it as a matter of fact.

Her old man, McAllister, gave me a different kind of look when he got there. You know, a *man* look. Like he was undressing me with his eyes. He kept zooming in on my boobs. Bet he was wondering what they looked like, my nipples in particular.

One of my johns once told me they looked like rosebuds. Not the flower kind I don't mean. But probably he could of meant those too perhaps 'cause he was always leaving me flowers of some kind or another. He was one of my regulars. Anyway he told me they looked like chocolate rosebuds. I think Rowntree makes them or something, little swirly chocolates that melt in your mouth.

That was the first job I ever had. It gave me a lot of experience.

Everybody used to always say I was pretty developed for a girl of twelve. I'd been getting my periods regular for about two years already and all the guys in school wanted to go out with me. They only wanted me for my body, but I didn't care 'cause it was more important to be popular.

Eddy is the guy I first went out with from high school. My first real boyfriend you could say. He was always trying to get me to go all the way. We had lots of fun without it so why bother I said to Eddy. He pushed me when we bummed days off school and he pushed me when we were rolling around in the back of his van at all hours of the night. On the day I told him I was taking the pill 'cause the doctor said I had to on account of some abnormality, Eddy got the pushiest ever.

He said, "That's great, little girl. Just super. No problems, no worries, let's do it."

"Okay," I said, "go ahead."

After a while he told me his friends wanted a piece of the action too 'cause the girlfriends of his friends weren't as nice and as generous as me. The parents of these girls were super strict and never cut them any slack.

"No way, hosay. I'm gonna get a reputation."

He told me never mind about that. There were perks to being famous. He told me how much money we could make and what we could buy with it.

"We could get you out of that shithole and away from your shithole foster parents. I'll buy you all the dope you can smoke and a month's worth of panties with the days of the week written on them."

So I said, "Okay."

It wasn't that bad really 'cause I never had to lie there for more than five minutes. Jesus were they ever horny. I'd lie there practicing my multiplication tables. Never got past somewhere around eight times seven equals fifty-six and that only happened the one time with a fat porker of a bald guy who was pissed out of his tree.

Twenty bucks a pop and a girl gets to liking that kinda dough pretty quick, not that Eddy ever gave me the whole twenty bucks. Pretty soon I heard of a way to make even more and that was by going independent.

When my lover boy started to pimp for some other chicks I broke up with him and went to stand on Dalhousie where the real action was. At the very beginning nobody took me seriously. Some cars slowed down, some construction guys whistled. But that's about it. It was becoming clear to me you couldn't succeed by doing this half-assed so I quit school just like I quit Eddy. I was flunking most things anyway, every subject except math.

I started to plaster my face with goopy make-up like the

pros and to wear ugly dresses so people passing by knew I meant business. It worked.

Most of the tricks were pretty revolting and stank. They just went at it, zipped in and out pretty damn quick like they had nothing better to do at that particular time of day or night, except for the one sweet guy who said, "Your nipples look like rosebuds." He never did it with me. Not even once. Not even nearly.

He wanted to see me topless and he told me he would pay the same rate. When he saw my tits it was like he was hypnotized or something and he told me they were just what he was looking for. Can you believe it, just what he was looking for.

"Two little chocolate rosebuds are what you have. I know this is going to sound kind of kinky, nevertheless — "

I loved it when he used that word on me, *nevertheless*. It made me feel real important for once. Like he was using words on me that would be good enough for Lady Di.

"I'd like to try various flavours out on you." *Various*, he said.

One day he covered me with whipped cream and licked it all off with his tongue. The next day it was honey. Then came the jam. Then shit I don't remember all the wacky things he did. Except for this one time he put a marashino cherry on each nipple.

I told him that they reminded me of two seals' noses balancing two little red beach balls and we both started to giggle and the cherries went rolling off and then just like that he started to bawl. I couldn't believe it and I kinda felt sorry for him. I really did 'cause everything he tried on me kinda felt really good. Better than most things. What I mean is he never sweated or grunted or swore or breathed heavy and he always remembered to leave me these flowers. Just because he liked my chocolate rosebuds.

CHOCOLATE ROSEBUDS

McAllister stood there gawking at me with these big bloodshot eyeballs and in my imagination I thought two holes should of been cut in my t-shirt. The better to see my nipples. I thought I'd of been better off wearing a wet t-shirt to this interview. It would of saved him all the trouble of trying to figure out what they looked like. Believe me I'd of flashed them in no time flat if the kids hadn't shown up or if I hadn't opened my big mouth first and said: "If you really want to know, they look like rosebuds. Chocolate ones."

As soon as I said it I knew I'd lost them. Both her and him and the job too. Mrs. McAllister had her two sons wrapped in her arms like as if she believed I was gonna molest them or something. So to get myself out of a real scrape, I said, "Your sons' eyes look like chocolate rosebuds. Don't you think so?"

I thought it up on the spot and the McAllisters acted as if it was a really nice thing to say.

"What a nice thing to say," Mrs. McAllister said, smiling a perfect smile that lit up her face. Her smile was as perfect as her hair and dress. Beautiful clothes, beautiful house, beautiful life. Pretty soon we were all standing around in the hallway smiling. Including me.

I didn't want to blow it this time so I waited to be invited in. Jobs were hard to come by and even harder to keep, I'd heard that enough times. And it was hard to find exactly the right job. Really there were only two things I was qualified for. One of them was taking off my clothes and the other was understanding children.

Broken Windows

LUCY DRIFTS ON A PONTOON BOAT CARRYING NO LIFE PRESERVERS. Bats swoop over her head in the dark, gobbling the millions of mosquitoes. Alistair, whistling, isn't bothered by the bats or the bugs. He stands over the steering wheel in a classic nautical position, one eye to a telescope pointed out to sea. They are on the lookout for a cabin called The Bear's Lair.

Careful continues to dive off the side of the boat. Lucy asks Alistair if sheet lightning is as dangerous and as deadly as regular thunderbolts and he nods.

"Careful, Careful."

"Oh, Lucille," she calls, emerging from the deep and sputtering a stream of water and minnows from her lips, "you're so significant." Careful's hair is more turquoise and wavy than the water.

"The fish don't bite in this weather," Alistair says, reeling in his line, casting it out one last time in a long sideways arc.

He asks Lucy to pass him his tackle box. Compartments unfold like tiny jack-in-the-boxes. He tosses his lure in amongst an assortment of nuts, bolts, nails and screws, then covers them precisely and ceremoniously with a swatch of brocade torn from her favourite wing chair.

❖

The morning of Lucy's dream, Lucy walks her daughter Rebecca to school. More or less insistent construction images are popping in and out of her head, like impulses she would once have followed. Lucy slept through the alarm, breakfast and the schoolbus; Rebecca flew in with a plan of action, peeled all the blankets off her mother until she was seated and wide awake.

"Hello, hello? Anybody under here?" she called.

"But you're *not* here, are you?" Alistair yelled last night, in a much different tone, waving a hand in front of her eyes in an attempt to make her blink. He looked in cupboards, he looked in drawers. He unballed a pair of Lucy's socks and threw them on the floor. At the height of his frustration he glared in the fridge, then slammed the door so hard Lucy could hear glass jars rattling against one another inside.

Rebecca is eight years old and it is also the insides of things that interest her. The inner workings. The innards, as Alistair would say. Like the houses along their street. Who lives here and who lives there? Is this family like their family? Or is that family better? Lucy is waiting for the questions, for any question, from anyone. She can float for months on the sea of her emotions without coming up with any questions of her own.

The smell of autumn is in the air. Crispy leaves on sodden ground. Fallen pine needles. Moribund worms and rain. Rebecca takes Lucy's hand in order to tiptoe along the curb and avoid stepping on the lawns. Lucy thinks Rebecca doesn't so much need her for balance as she does for presence. She thinks Rebecca wants to assure herself Lucy has not disappeared altogether, the way she has vowed many times under her breath to do.

One house has a door, trim, and a fence the colour of eggnog. Still-in-bloom flowers, probably fake and tinted to match, fill the clay potters that sit on each of the three steps by the front door. The curled-up arms of the letterbox are laden with junk flyers and put her in mind of the dream she used to have, for three years after Rebecca was born. The one where she was carrying Rebecca's bloody body away from the scene of a car crash. Somebody home? Nobody home? It's hard for Lucy to tell.

The curb steers them to the left and they are on Moresby now.

All down the long avenue, rounded, well-stuffed Halloween garbage bags keep the earth from rising up in revolt. Lucy is positive this is what it yearns to do. On television the earth crumbles like glass struck by a hammer, and houses topple into it. News is delivered to her from behind the glass of her television set by an anchorwoman who is also her neighbour. Ever since she's lived here, Lucy has watched the anchorwoman speak the hot burbling lava that spews from volcanoes, lava that stretches over the land the way a teardrop might stretch over a face; the teardrop of a person well past either resistance or capitulation.

Witches, ghosts, corn stalks and black cats aplenty attempt to goad Lucy into shame over the ready-carved pumpkin she bought at J.C.'s Orchard and Nursery, and then forgot there at the cash. One house boasts seven pumpkins, each weighing over three hundred pounds. The driveway of another house is lined with tombstones that say R.I.P. Dracula, on a patio chair, cape open, flashes a t-shirt proclaiming life to be a bowl of bloody cherries.

One of three crows perched side by side on a light standard caws at the same time Rebecca begins to say something. Rebecca says this is significant. "Significant" is not a word she can pronounce correctly (she says *sifignicant* or *signicitant*) and since Rebecca has been taught its meaning by Alistair, Lucy doesn't bother to correct her. For Rebecca's sake, Lucy never disturbs the unit of father and daughter. She realizes that this might be for her own sake, in order to buy more time.

From the top of her coppery head to the arc of toes at her feet, the child has nothing that belongs to Lucy, nothing from the Lucy McBride gene pool. Rebecca grew inside her from a speck of nothing to a full-sized baby, feeding on what Lucy ate, relaxing to what Lucy planned for them. But there is nothing in or on Rebecca to prove this.

Rebecca looks up with Alistair's startling hazel eyes. Alistair's bell-shaped lips form bubbles of unintelligible words Lucy has neither the energy nor the desire to reach out and catch. Up above, the sky is scheduling a storm and Lucy hears herself suggesting they pick up the pace before they get soaked.

"I can't wait until tonight," Rebecca giggles, sidling up. "It's gonna be so spooky." There. Again. The adult teeth coming up with jagged, serrated tops, like the ineffectual blades of plastic knives, crowding Rebecca's mouth. For an instant Lucy smiles herself because Rebecca reminds her of the pumpkins everywhere. Then her oesophagus constricts like a sopping cloth being wrung out.

"You don't ever really get scared, do you?" Lucy asks. "There's nothing in the whole world a little girl has to be scared of."

"Somebody might take me. You know, a bad person." Then Rebecca would be somebody else, living in a different family in a different place. Inside another life.

Lucy tries to convince Rebecca that Alistair would never allow something like that to happen. He would comb the earth until he found her. "Your father would not rest one second until you were home, safe and sound." And while Alistair was out looking, Lucy would be lighting candles, saying prayers, comforting her in her dreams.

What an idea. To be taken. To be spirited away.

Lucy can see past all the houses. She can see the whole neighbourhood as it might look tomorrow and calculates how little their "wise" investment might be worth then. Egg yolk hardened upon the window panes. Toilet paper mummy-wrapped around the maple tree out front. The garage door spraypainted with obscenities. The driveway strewn with blood, paint, pumpkin guts and broken pumpkin shells.

Once, as a kid, on Halloween, she had thrown eggs at the doctors' houses by the hospital. Once, she had broken two bevelled glass windows of a Tudor style home. She had not felt guilty then, but alive and awake, as though the blood in her body had a destination, had some important purpose of its own. After being reprimanded, she sat down to catch her breath and assess the damage. She glimpsed the back of her hand, its veins swollen wondrously big and blue.

Rebecca is going trick-or-treating tonight with Alistair. It has been decided. Decided also, that Lucy will stay home and pass out candy, dressed for the event as the person she would secretly like to become. Rebecca threw something appropriate together for her mother when Lucy descended from the attic with nothing more than a plastic skeleton mask. Rebecca presented her with a long, silvery white, layered evening gown which waved and shimmered as Lucy moved, like the gossamer tails of tiny goldfish.

Costume settled, Alistair had said, "Perfect." Lucy was perfect, the day was perfect, their family was perfect, they lived in a perfect house — the house he'd always dreamed of. His dream home. His enthusiasm was genuine, but not contagious.

In fifteen years Lucy and Alistair have gone from a condo to a town home to a thirty-four-hundred square-foot single in a neighbourhood where the celebrities from television, radio and government chose to live. The McBride backyard was kitty corner, in fact, to the backyard of the anchorwoman for the midday news show.

"I like the way the anchorwoman keeps her house. It looks so lived in," Lucy has said to Alistair. "And it has a pool, with a deep end, and a diving board." At night, from May to October, when not even a sleeping pill can deliver Lucy to sleep, Lucy watches her neighbour frogstroke from end to end of that pool, as light as an insect, as sleek as a thread. A woman who has made something of herself and who knows the trick to enjoying it. Maybe Lucy and Alistair could look into getting a pool.

"Not until Spring of 1998," Alistair replied. "Our money goes to the *inside* of the house first, then we'll see."

Lucy's house is so big it echoes. The house is so quiet it deafens her. Its size and its silence sicken her, oppress her and yet all she can think to do is hurry back to it, draw the blinds in her bedroom and fling herself into a sleep that will make the days and nights pass quickly. Every step is an effort to stay afloat. She is so tired.

Once at the school grounds, Lucy hands Rebecca her knapsack and lunch box. Before Lucy can kiss her, Rebecca is away.

"Away you go," Lucy calls as Rebecca loses herself in a flurry of colours and moving bodies which burn Lucy's eyes.

Children are tussling at the top of the play structure, impatiently waiting their turns to whiz down the yellow tube slide. A chorus of high-pitched voices drums into Lucy's ears; she plugs her ears with her fingers, turns her back on the noise. Through this she can still make out Rebecca's singsong, although it has become urgent.

"Mom! Mom!"

A big orange school bus has missed Lucy by inches. The driver is beeping the horn. Lucy stands there impassively, watching the bus move into the distance.

❖

"Watch how long I can hold my breath under water, Lucille," says Careful.

Lucy refuses to give in to her daughter's wishes and continues to walk around the island, dogged by the squelch of rubber and her own huge footprints. She's on the verge of a scream, a roar, to get Careful's voice out of her head, when Careful plummets off a bridge into the rapids below where she lands with a cannonball splash. Adult-sized Lucy is the one pushed against the current. The water tastes like the warm milk Lucy drinks before bed; her lips turn purple from the cold in the air.

Suddenly she is on her livingroom couch, it is covered with loam and plaster chunks. Scrolls of wallpaper samples, tied in red ribbon, fill the vase on the coffee table. Beside them is a tub of drywall compound, already mixed, and a row of paintbrushes in ascending order, from smallest to biggest. Alistair, hammer in hand, is nailing colonial baseboard and quarter round above the gritty, pumice-coloured foundation. Above him, along the ceiling, he has just affixed the egg and dart moulding.

"What do you think of a chandelier?" he is impatient to know.

"Yes," she says, "a chandelier is a definite must."

❖

"What goes in goulash?" Lucy asks Rebecca who is standing on a kitchen chair, already in her costume, beside Alistair and helping him cook. Rebecca is passing ingredients into his outstretched palm. He sprinkles them in the frying pan.

"Dad says anything but the kitchen sink," Rebecca answers. "Right, Dad?"

"Right, Kiddo."

Back in the seventies, Lucy could make a pretty mean gazpacho. Deadly Parker House rolls. Rebecca says she can't believe that, can't believe that her mother ever cooked, but the sparkle in her eyes and her pumpkin smile tells Lucy that she does believe, or at least that she would like to, more than anything.

"Back in the seventies, your mother could do a lot of things," Alistair tells Rebecca.

"So what goes in gazpacho then?" Rebecca asks Lucy.

"Gazpacho." Lucy tries to flavour the word with a bit of Spanish accent. "Let me think a minute."

"Paprika," Alistair says, his palm empty and waiting again.

"It's eaten cold, you know," Lucy offers. "And the way I used to serve it was inside ripe summer tomatoes. Hollowed out to double as soup bowls."

Sitting at the table, blindly flipping the pages of Alistair's *Globe And Mail*, Lucy tells Rebecca that they, her and Alistair, used to eat it often in their tiny rented apartment, the one they had before they finished university. Poor as church mice, they owned a folding card table, two lawn chairs, a black and white TV with rabbit ears, a book shelf with dimestore Tolstoys, Dostoevskys, Kafkas, Chekhovs. And an air mattress for a bed.

For curtains they pinned up old tablecloths or sheets from the Neighbourhood Services. And they didn't own many dishes, except chipped ones and ones that didn't match, so the tomato bowls had come in handy.

"Those were the days," Alistair says and offers Rebecca a taste of goulash from the wooden spoon. "Your mother was quite a rising star on campus. She was failing *Introduction To Logic*, but she could belt out an ode or a eulogy on the spot for her devoted following of students and faculty. Most of them believed we were in the midst of a genuine prophet. Kahlil Gibran and JoJo the Psychic rolled into one. They would stalk me just to get close to her. Some would work up the nerve to ask me what it was like to live close to a mind like hers. 'She's just Lucy,' I would tell them."

"I want to be a writer like Mom," Rebecca declares proudly.

"Hey, Pumpkin," Alistair says, "I thought you wanted to be an architect. I don't think there's a building on this planet that ever got built with anything as flimsy as words. Go ahead, name me one."

Past the family room, through the sliding patio doors, Lucy can see the anchorwoman's house, its outline distinctly visible against the backdrop of swiftly fallen night. This evening there is a fluorescent moon, full and round. Lucy can see right into the anchorwoman's kitchen, can see the family — three boys, the woman and her husband — sitting on stools around a wooden island.

In the center on a lazy-susan there is a pizza in a cardboard box. The anchorwoman passes out pieces on floppy plates. The boys scramble and tussle and tug at what must be a long thread of cheese and she, in response, tries to wrap their knuckles with the spatula.

Lucy stands. If she watches the family long enough, some of their mirth is sure to infect her. Like standing in front of a mirror for fifteen minutes, with nothing but a resolute smile so that your facial muscles start to send happy messages to your brain. Ask Alistair. There is always some trick to help you out of a jam, always an answer for everything. "Every problem has a solution if you would just use your head," he has advised her. "Try something. Crunch some numbers. Find some worthy goal to focus on."

A noise issues from behind, calling back her attention. Rebecca has slipped off her chair and already been scooped up by Alistair who has resumed the supervision of his cooking. Rebecca's arms are around his neck and her legs around his lower back. Daddy's girl. At intervals he plants kisses on her forehead.

At this moment, Lucy wishes she had a reliable afternoon lover whose arms she could run into. A man with strong, rescusitating arms which could squeeze the sleep out of her. A man who could give her a loving and affectionate Heimlich Manoeuvre so that the clogging pit of sleep would project itself onto some other surface, into some other host.

She slept with the man who came to clean the furnace last year. It had had no impact.

Lucy shuffles to the basement door and is halfway down the stairs before Alistair calls, "No supper?"

"Not hungry."

"You know that's not good for you."

"Holler when you're leaving. I'll come up and have a bite," she says, though she knows that's not likely. Likely, when he leaves, she'll turn out all the lights and pretend nobody's home.

Downstairs she zigzags past all the construction materials, threads her way through all the upright framing to an alcove way at the back, one tenth the size of the whole area. Alistair has cordoned this section off for her to do hobbies. The larger part of the basement is to be transformed into a bedroom, complete with shower and toilet, a TV room, an office with fireproof safe for all their important documents — deed, insurance, will, receipts. For tax purposes, she is supposed to say everything down here is for her and for her "business".

She sits at her table, reaches behind her and pulls the chain cord to turn on the light. Glue gun in hand, she begins to fasten paisley ribbons to wreaths of twine, twine that looks like the brambles in her garden when the snow comes. She takes up some dried flowers and wires them through the twine with a pair of needlenose pliers. A few sprinkles of the liquid from her mason jar and everything has the raspberry fragrance of a rose, even here in the musty underground. She steps back a few steps to view her creations and thinks them not half bad. If more light filtered through the two windows, she could judge them more severely.

Alistair stomps on the floor above her, three times with his big heavy foot. "Come on, Lucy, come and get it while it's hot."

Loud. Angry. He has run out of words for his frustration with her. Good. Drawers are slamming. There is finality in the brattle of cutlery. What will come next she has no idea, but something, a deeply felt instinct, warns her that she must remain down here, silent, pushing against the two-by-fours with all her weight. Pushing Alistair beyond his limit.

He calls a few more times and she ignores him. "You can starve for all I care," he shouts. "I don't give a rat's ass. I'm way beyond giving a rat's anything anymore. Way beyond."

Limply she swings around a beam, holding to it with one hand, trusting it will hold her. She begins to swing around the other ones, skipping to a voice that's calling out squares in her head. On her fourth or fifth partner, the palm of her hand slams into a protruding nail. Without looking, Lucy merely registers that it is her right hand and not her left, the one she used to write with. She pulls herself free.

Her back leans against the wood; she slides down and sits. Warm blood emerges between her palm and the cold cement floor, then forms a pretty pattern around her white fingers. The pattern is like the chalk lines around dead bodies at the murder scenes on the news. Like the ones at suicide scenes probably, although these are never shown.

Lucy has never been able to stomach the sight of blood or the knowledge of her own mortality — this is what she thinks just before consciousness ebbs away.

❖

At the construction trailer the sign warns in dramatic red letters HARD HATS AND SAFETY BOOTS MUST BE WORN ON SITE. *An engine starts up and Alvin, the foreman, points to buttons he can press and sticks he can pull inside his bulldozer.*

Out of Lucy's housecoat comes a wrinkled list of the things he will have to look at come inspection time. Nail pops, hairline cracks, buckles in the linoleum, a wasp's nest hanging from the eaves.

"Not to worry," Alvin says, "the value of your house has gone up ten grand already and it's only been a year. I told you, Señora Baudelaire. That's the great thing about buying at pre-construction prices, before we have a chance to slap up any models."

Alistair pulls up in his cement truck, its torso churning. He has enough hot chocolate and marshmallows for the entire crew and a blueprint rolled up under one arm.

"We have a problem," he says and spits. "Sewer people put a lean on us and everything's at a bloody standstill."

"That's not what the Mrs. says," says Alvin, every other tooth missing from his smile.
Alistair spots Lucy. "What are you doing here?"

❖

A relentless succession of trick-or-treaters materializes to ring the doorbell and open pillow cases, into which Lucy doles out her offerings of suckers, gum and candy kisses. For the youngest, decked out in the most complete and convincing finery, she drops double helpings. To children whose voices or parents she recognizes, she says, "An extra special something if you can guess who I'm supposed to be." Whatever they say — beautiful lady, fairy, angel, mermaid — wins them one of Lucy's homemade wreaths. Wreaths she is supposed to sell next week at the craft fair in the mall. Buoy-shaped wreaths to hang over their beds, she tells them now, to keep them from drowning in their dreams.

At about eight-thirty, when things have quieted to a trickle, she opens the door before a knock or the bell, having watched three people come up the driveway.

"Trick or treat, smell my feet, give me something good to eat. Not too big, not too small, just the size of Montreal."

Pleased with their chant, the two boys punch each other. The anchorwoman, in a trenchcoat, ear muffs and red woollen mittens, smiles at Lucy, and rolls her eyes back. Both of them hers, the anchorwoman is ashamed to say. The other one is at home daring kids to thrust their hands into a pail of boiled spaghetti noodles which he bills as the ghoulish entrails and brains of a corpse. Any taker brave enough to plunge in receives a movie coupon from the video store where he works.

"Hi," she says, extending her mittened hand over the tops of her sons' heads. "Nancy Ciprianno. I'm right behind you, in the white high-ranch."

"I've seen you," Lucy says. "Around, and on the news."

The anchorwoman pats the head of each boy. Jason is the vampire; the werewolf is Jordan. "Tell these wise guys," she says to Lucy, "that they have to earn their candy. Make them dance a jig or recite a poem. Make them sing a song."

"There was a man from Nantucket," the older of the boys says.

The anchorwoman places her hand over his mouth, saying he has a sense of humour this one, saying evidently she can dress him up but not take him anywhere. She releases her grip and he launches into a rendition of "Roses Are Red, Violets Are Blue" which neither rhymes nor makes sense.

"My reputation ruined in one fell swoop. Fabulous, guys, just fabulous." The anchorwoman jokes that her whole life — job, house, husband, kids — is up for sale. "Dirt cheap."

Lucy puts in off-handedly that, you never know, the anchorwoman could have a writer on her hands, to make her proud. This is exactly, she says, how she got *her* start. Scribbling in a duo-tang at the age of nine, nonsense poems about boys she loved who didn't love her back. "Unrequited love."

"You're a poet?" the anchorwoman asks excitedly. "Published?"

Lucy gathers her hair into a ponytail and holds it with one hand as she passes out candy with the other. She nods while her head is down. "A chapbook. It was nothing. It was a long time ago."

"Wait until I tell my husband. Do you know I've spent most of my working life wanting to be as glamorous as Anne Sexton? When I'm reading the news every day do you know who I'm pretending to be? Anne Sexton — high as a kite in a long evening gown with a cigarette between my fingers, dishing out a version of reality that hasn't been dressed up in a better evening gown than the one I'm wearing." She laughs. "Really, a poet, eh?" She stands back, taking in from head to toe Lucy's costume, which is being battered like a flag in rough winds. Summarily, she says, "A poetess."

"And still living. But just barely," Lucy announces, holding up her gauze-bandaged hand.

Goodnights and thank yous are exchanged along with pledges to have coffee and chat. The wound does not arouse any pity or concern. The anchorwoman has seen it all, Lucy supposes, or, the wound is considered a part of the costume. Nothing more than a prop to yield a clue about Lucy's identity. The older boy had guessed bride, then on spotting her hand, bride of Frankenstein. But the anchorwoman's comment had been decisive. Poetess.

Alistair had wrapped Lucy's hand carefully, and with the tender ministrations she had once mistaken for love. For some reason he had decided to check on her before heading out with Rebecca. On discovering Lucy folded up on the cold cement floor, he had known, as always, what to do. He carried her to the main level, waved an ammonia pellet under her nose, dabbed at her hand with cotton balls dipped in hydrogen peroxide, wrapped her hand in gauze, checked her immunization card to verify the date of the last tetanus shot. Blood was transferred in the press of palms.

Alistair was all set to drive Lucy to Emergency, but Lucy said no, not to be silly. Then he would stay home. Children would never forgive a parent's pain on such an important night as this, Lucy had said. She convinced him by dressing in her costume and by greeting the first of her Halloween arrivals. See, she wouldn't bleed to death. See. She promised. Bleeding to death, at the rate she was bleeding, would take years.

And all things considered, she isn't sure she has that many

left. Before, at least, she often had to fight the urge to rouse Alistair in the night, to hurt him by scraping her fingers down the length of his back. Her touch always stopped short over his confidently breathing body or on it, startled by the bone beneath his skin. When she spotted his eyes in a long flutter beneath the lids or when she was struck by the electric twitch of his muscles, she was tempted to smother him with a pillow. To separate him from dreams he did not permit her to enter, the way she might enter a poem or a house. Alistair will not be entered like this. Now she accepts, Alistair will not be entered.

Out the window, stiffened leaves skitter across the pavement like wind-up toys on their way to work, like actors in a movie that is set on fast forward, racing toward the credits. Despite its slits for eyes, the moon is spying on the goings-on below. Perhaps the moon is God, stalking potential victims she hopes to alter with her incomparable magnetic pull. A girl slightly older than Rebecca will begin later tonight to menstruate. A couple, crazed by a cannibalistic lust, will conceive the child heretofore inconceivable. A man who otherwise walks the earth in a good suit and with sensible leather shoes will sprout hairs, claws and fangs, suddenly becoming aware of the obscene, beggarly scent of a female and he will follow it miraculously, quite miraculously, for miles.

For Lucy, outside on the porch now in her bare feet, the scent of possibility is carried along the gelid air currents or along the warm moonbeams which seem to swathe her in chaste kisses. Possibility lies somewhere inside the pumpkin which she scrapes until the meat is embedded under her fingernails, until she has gathered enough guts to make a salve for her wound.

She stands right where the anchorwoman stood and tries to envision herself through the anchorwoman's eyes. She cannot. Backing up, to see if she can see more clearly, she notices the archway of the front door, perfectly sharp in its angles. She finds herself trying to remember if this is a safe place to hide during an earthquake, or not. On the news she has heard where it is you are supposed to hide: it is under a door or under a desk.

What she has never heard is where to situate yourself if you want to see everything up close. If your goal is to stand at some appointed place while the earth crumbles and turns in on itself, glass and rubble and damage stretching in all directions, for miles and miles, farther than the eye can see.

Mary With The Cool Shades

THE WIZENED OLD MARY, STEEPED IN THE SMELL OF URINE AND loving it, shrieks out obscenities I'd have never ascribed to women of her generation, never ascribed to women period. Her language shocks me, as much as it did when my father used it on my mother, and my mother didn't use it back.

"Fuck you. Go fuck yourself, you cocksucking little bastard."

Mary wears a pink nylon housecoat, knitted booties on her feet, an assortment of jewellery — a rhinestone brooch, rings, clip-ons, a choker with a cameo, its white maidenly head sharp against the black of the velvet. On her lap she has an evening purse which she opens and closes daintily, with purpose. She has positioned herself in the middle of things where visitors, me included, will have to slow down, go around, be recognized perhaps, judging from the way she perches in her wheelchair.

Black sunglasses deaden her eyes.

"Does Mary want her tea today?" asks one of the nurses.

"Or not?"

"You drink it, you trollop. You nasty bugger."

"Oh, the way you go on, Mary," the nurse says. "What would we ever do without our Mary? Our Mary with the cool shades."

I'm staring at Mary in a way I know is impolite, encouraged by her absurd fashion sense and the vulgarity of her language. Here sits a woman who doesn't know the difference anyway. I have determined that because of the chair Mary must be helpless, because of the glasses, blind.

"How's your life, dear?" she suddenly puts to me. "Still clotting?"

She has applied her strength to the arms of her chair in an effort to make herself look imposing, this despite the way her age proffers her clavicles and restrains the dough of her body.

My face reddens, and the nurse tells me to pay Mary no mind. "Though she gets to the heart of things, she does," the nurse allows. "In double jig time, don't you, Mary?"

Mary whinnies with delight at the nurse, then turns her face away and spits.

❖

Down the hall, my mother lies almost sleeping, in a sliver of sunlight. All the patients with broken bones, women mostly with white hair, and as still as the dead, have distracted me from the approach to her bed. I've taken the time to ask myself which of these two for the occasion: an aspect of sympathy or a look of bright cheer?

I teetered momentarily between the two alternatives and then entered her room with a phoney trademark smile.

The sheets are pulled up to her chin so that only her head is revealed, white skin and white hair on a white pillow. Sleepy head, I think. If not for the arches of her still-brown eyebrows my mother's face might be altogether invisible. It is drained of any colour it once possessed. Even on Sunday mornings, a long time ago, after night-long arguments with my father, when I'd crawl into bed beside her trying to hurry breakfast along, her eyes would be dusted a soft green. There would be a blush of peach powder on her cheeks and faintly smudged red darkening her lips. "Nobody who looks as pretty as you should sleep the day away," I'd tell her.

Mary's cursing and whinnying grow louder, even though they are echoing down a very long hall.

"Tell them to shut her up," my mother says. "I'd like to get a little rest if that's possible. Go get the doctor, my medication's wearing off."

I ring for help, knowing from my experience with ulcers that nobody's likely to respond in a hurry. It sounds as though Mary is causing quite a disturbance and several room bells are ringing already. There's no help in sight. A result of cutbacks probably, the patients and my mother are expected to fend for themselves.

"Didn't I ask you to do something for me? It's not brain surgery, it's one simple task. If I could walk, you know, I'd have done it myself."

My mother has fallen down those stairs she keeps cluttered with clothes, boxes, garbage; she has broken her ankle. Quite badly, I'm told by the surgeon. From what I understand, it happened around eight o'clock and she waited all night with an insistent blade of bone sticking out of her foot. She waited for the sound of my key in the door so she could scream from the bottom of the stairs, letting me know just how long she'd waited, begrudging me every second I wasn't there to rescue her. She lay there all night, I'm certain of it, concentrating on the pain, not making a single sound, trying to pinpoint the transition from darkness to light, which I could have told her is imperceptible. Like watching people grow.

It's a question I can hear her asking me: "When does darkness give way to light?" Expecting me to know the answer and tell her. "Is that something everyone knows except me? Figures."

If I could, I would tell her. I would tell her there is a God who doesn't have it in for her, that she serves some purpose in this life beyond her suffering. But how to make someone see what their heart is set against?

I know she loves me.

My mother sends me cards on every holiday of the year and they're all signed in big generous letters, LOVE ALWAYS, MOM. She brags to her friends that I come by to visit her every morning with doughnuts and coffee before we head off to the bus stop together, and to work. In her wallet is a newspaper clipping that says I came in second in the Miss Ottawa Valley Beauty Pageant. Everybody is to understand having come in second is pretty terrific, infinitely better than coming in third.

What I want from her is something more, something Jack tells me is impossible and to forget. I want words from her, straight talk. Talk like Mary's that goes to the heart of things. I know those words are in my mother even though she claims to be no good with them. They've been forced deep inside her by a man who didn't allow her to speak, but they're in there. Sometimes I think she expects me to reach in and get them because she knows that I know they're there.

Sometimes I think she hates me for knowing that instead of knowing how to help her.

When Jack catches me racing from one thing to another, running myself ragged, he stands in the middle of our house, quoting from my father's A.A. prayer — ACCEPT THE THINGS YOU CANNOT CHANGE. ACCEPT THE THINGS YOU CANNOT CHANGE. And he doesn't stop, until I do.

MARY WITH THE COOL SHADES

❖

I come here every day to visit my mother. It's been five days and I haven't missed. There's nobody else. Not even Jack because he has just started a new job and can't get the time off. Every day she asks me why Jack can't come, says it's a shame Jack couldn't be here.

Usually I find her in the smoking lounge and my habit is to wait in a chair stashed by the exit and watch her through the glass until she finishes. My mother's not the kind of woman to be rushed. She signals to me she'll be another moment as messages and medicines hurtle forth in a tube that runs along the ceiling. And then she comes forward crookedly, untalented on her new crutches.

Today she's lying flat and resolutely in bed. She's no longer going to try, she tells me. She's giving up.

"What does the doctor say?" I ask.

"I can't go home until I can walk with the sticks and that includes being able to manage up and down stairs."

"Maybe we could rent you a wheelchair."

She takes this as a reproach — me telling her she should have drunk her milk, me telling her she should have exercised more (especially to develop that upper body strength), me telling her she should have taken her hormone pills, me telling her she should have taken better care of herself.

"Funny what the lucky think of the ignorant," she says.

Her room is full of flowers and cards, a fruitbasket from the people she works with. There have been complaints the fruits are attracting flies, but she just leaves it there on the window sill, the bananas freckling, the fruitflies suspended and dangling like tiny baubles on a mobile.

Across from my mother's bed a nurse cradles an old woman's

head; with her free hand the nurse brushes her hair. She pounds, she tugs. The old woman seems content to be manipulated in this way. I can see myself, if my mother ever comes to require such care, brushing so much more carefully, in deference to the fragility of what lies between us. I couldn't brush her hair the way I wanted to, not that I know which way that would be.

"You know that Mary person who's keeping us all awake with her yackety-yack and racket?" my mother asks. "I want you to go shoot her. Put her out of my misery."

Somebody, I assume it's Mary, is playing "Happy Birthday" on an electronic keyboard, singing loudly off-key.

The woman does whatever she feels like and the world doesn't fall down. "You have to hand it to Mary," I tell my mother.

I want to hear what my mother really thinks of Mary. For the past few nights I've dreamt of the old woman and for the past few mornings, written about her in my journal, maybe because my mother used to wear sunglasses herself years ago, even around the house. No woman in my mother's day could pull off wearing such things, except for maybe Jacqueline Kennedy Onassis. Everybody knew why Mrs, O'Byrne was wearing them, especially when she was likewise wearing long-sleeved blouses and dresses in the sweltering heat of summer.

If I say nothing and suggest indifference, I imagine I might be able to delay my mother here and pry something loose.

"The whole staff standing around with nothing better to do than to listen to the likes of Mary. Mary and her music. Mary who got left by Clarke Somebody-or-other and who told him what's what. Mary swearing like a trooper. Nobody ever listens to *me*. Fuck you, fuck you. See, I've been taking lessons."

My mother stares at the nurse across from her, still brushing the old woman's hair. My mother hopes to get a response. She turns her glare on me. I don't know what to say either. Maybe if she'd sounded more convincing. Maybe if she's spoken like Mary, with a little of Mary's pizzazz.

❖

Mary is in my path when visiting hours are over. She's hunched over her evening purse, spittle suspended finely from mouth to chest. Mary looks dead while giving off the sweet smell of sherry. I break the filament of spit and wipe her lips with my thumb. Mary doesn't thank me. Mary doesn't have to.

The walk to the parking lot is slow. The drive home is slow. Ordinarily I have a talent for making time move quickly by doing things without stopping to think about them, as though individual moments are solid things I can catch and simply throw away. In the car however, from the hospital to my mother's house, I can't seem to do it. Every house looks like the one before. The setting sun is always ahead of me. The clock barely registers movement. For whose benefit is all this lack of rushing, I wonder. For mine or my mother's?

Inside, I can see Jack has moved my mother's bed into the livingroom for the remainder of her convalescence. Anticipating the prognosis, he has already procured a wheelchair, folded it and leaned it in the corner. He has left a few dishes for me to wash, but has done me the favour of tidying up. For this surprise I wish to kiss and hug him.

My bedroom is exactly the way it was the day I married Jack, posters of teenage idols still taped to the wall. My mother is keeping everything for me in case I ever decide to come home. I've suggested the house is too big for one person, that she should find herself a little apartment near a bank and grocery store, something that would require less upkeep. She says she couldn't do that, Jack and I might get a divorce. Only one out of every two marriages lasts and given we have no children to unite us, the odds are doubly stacked against us.

I couldn't sleep in a single bed ever again. I'd toss and turn like a storm that can't find sky. It is from my little single bed with no one to comfort me or guard me from predatory nightmares that I listened to fists pummelling surfaces. If I'm going to perish now, it's by sinking into the valley at the centre of my double mattress at home, the place where two warm bodies have converged and loved with something fierce enough to wake the dead.

So, I will only close my eyes in this house for a rest.

Back downstairs, I smooth the wrinkles on my mother's bed in the livingroom, lie on top to consider what's coming. My mother will be arriving home sooner or later with useless crutches. She will be in a wheelchair. She will depend on me to help her and I will try to do my best. The wheelchair will be in the way and I'll have to get around it somehow.

Brittle bones.

My mother.

Mary.

I start to get a picture of them together, sitting side by side. Having to talk to one another makes them both uncomfortable — they have nothing in common but a pair of sunglasses and perhaps not even *they* understand that — so in my mind I send them back centuries. To an earlier time and to a livelier place where, even outnumbered by men and overpowered by the lack of opportunities, Mary would fit right in and show herself to be a lady who knows how to take control.

My heart is hammering away in my chest when Mary begins to punch on piano keys. Everyone listening to her seems eager, tense; they clamour for her attention. Her booties tap to the beat. She smiles a fiendish smile and downs the shot of whiskey kept above her on the piano. Cowboys ride into town, trail dust into her smoke-filled saloon and they hoist themselves on the stools and toss coins at her cleavage. They applaud lustily when Mary feigns collaboration. She wears her cool shades, black and deep, the sharpness of what shows of her face converging knowingly on her patrons, one here, one there. These cowboys need her, want her, but they will never touch her.

My mother is over in the corner. An indigo dress creeps outward in a flounce and its shading offsets the whiteness of her skin. Indigo feathers fan out elegantly from her hair. She's enjoying the music, and is gathering momentum to get up and dance by herself on the table. She's beautiful and happy, but a little afraid she'll falter if Mary's fingers stop making music.

I am also afraid. My heart is beating too fast, skipping beats. The last thing I want is to find myself in this picture so I squeeze my eyes very tight. I try to keep the livingroom light from filtering into the light of the saloon.

Her Industry Of Lies

LILAH NEVER WOULD HAVE MARRIED ARTIE IF SHE'D KNOWN about his wooden leg. This is what she tells herself: I never would have hooked up with the likes of Artie if my father hadn't gone off and left me at fifteen with a dying mother and three kid brothers to look after. Never. This is what she tells herself although it is not what she tells the now dead mother. In a million years, never, is the way she puts it. She's emphatic on this point. Artie was eleven inches shorter and what's more, he belted her around like nobody's business.

Lilah had never been attracted to him during their courtship; however, her height being what it was (six feet tall in flats) and her prospects being what they were (negligible to nil), she took the advice of her brother Ernest who said, "Let Artie chase you until you catch him. Artie's no prize," he added, "but if we're speaking the truth, Lilah, neither are you."

The first time Artie asked her out, it was to a dance.

"You limp," she snorted.

"It's temporary," he assured her.

At seven o'clock that evening he fetched her strawberry punch and dabbed at her lip, between sips, with a monogrammed handkerchief. At eight he twirled and dipped her in front of the barber shop quartet. Under the porchlight at nine, with Lilah's brothers spying from the top bunk in their bedroom, he placed a kiss on her forehead, between her eyes. A gentle breeze passed by, cooling the imprint of the kiss, sealing it, and at that moment she knew, she just knew, he'd make a dandy father. He couldn't miss.

Five months later, when she modestly emerged from the bathroom on her wedding night in a checked flannel nightgown, buttons done up to her chin, Artie removed his leg and swung it like a baseball bat across her backside.

It was a hell of a wallop, but she barely flinched.

"Three strikes," he warned, "and you're out."

❖

Though Lilah hid her bruises with compact powder and turtle necks so the neighbours wouldn't talk or ask questions, eventually, in private, she came to gaze at them in the full length swivel dressing mirror. Sometimes she would tip the mirror forward and fling it back so that the image of herself, naked and multi-coloured, would rock and loom, shrink and vanish, as she repeated over and over to herself, "He loves me. He loves me not." Sometimes she would cheat so it stopped on the right answer.

Lilah had been the only one in the family her father didn't smack. Until Artie came along she'd gone through life feeling invisible. Soon, with her hands, she would learn to climb and toboggan all over the welts accumulating on her backside. She would insert her fingers inside herself, feel the liquid there and think of it drowning her useless good grades, good manners and good deeds. The spasms between her legs were like a pulse by which she could keep time, by which she could be sure time existed and was moving her along.

Artie walked in on her once and threw a conniption.

"Nobody touches you except me. You got that, woman?"

He undid his belt. He unzipped his fly. His pants dropped around his ankles, the real and the wooden.

He'd made it through the previous night without grinding his teeth so she worked up the courage to say, "Your poor leg, Artie, don't get yourself in a tizzy."

"The long and the short of it is," he told her, "I lost this leg over a woman who thought she could do as she pleased and I'll not lose this other the same way."

Lilah suspected he'd lost his limb to something like gangrene or cancer, but ten would get her twenty at the racetrack that some of the things he said just HAD to be true.

"Did she egg you on, Artie? That other woman?"

"Keep it up and you'll find out where that got her."

❖

Artie's pet name for Lilah was "Miss Goody Two Shoes". Lilah gave up trying to figure out if he had it in for her because she'd grown up Catholic, or for having both feet. Instead she made an effort to behave badly and walk with an outstep so pronounced, in platform shoes so ridiculous, people would wonder how in Hell's half acre a man like Artie could get himself saddled to a beanstalk like her.

Who cared what her brothers had to say? Who cared what those biddies whispered about her over at the coin wash? As far as she was concerned, everybody else could go scrub.

Artie could get sozzled and smash beer bottles in the kitchen — would she care? A wail of police sirens could slip through the three holes at the bottom of the storm windows — would she bring herself to go have a look? The cry of a colicky baby could rise above the din of the inside and the outside — would she approach to be the good mother? No to all of them. Not on her life. She had never in her life felt more at peace. Yes, that is correct, never.

Ernest HAD NOT been laid off from the mill. Roger HAD NOT been charged with theft. Gus WAS NOT living over the poolroom with a woman old enough to be his grandmother. Gladioli DID spring up of themselves in droves of purple and red and white over her mother's grave, summer through winter, and she DID NOT have to travel forty miles every Sunday afternoon to tend them.

When Artie staggered in, belched and said, "Take the rugrat for a walk, Miss Goody Goody," it was exactly the same as having him say, "No doubt about it, my sweet, there's not the slightest way I could manage without you."

❖

Lilah's mother had made her swear to keep the boys together and remain their guardian until they either married, became priests, or got sick and died of the cancer that ran on her side, or the lunacy that ran on their father's.

"You're my best and my brightest, and I'm counting on you."

Lilah promised, crossed her heart.

"Don't you ever let those boys forget where they come from. You remind them about their father — his temper, his gambling, his chasing skirts. The world doesn't need one more like your father. One like your father is plenty for this world."

Lilah was to make do on her own and never run back to that rodent for a red cent.

As soon as her mother was safely tucked in, her tombstone like a headboard behind her, Lilah quit school and took a job at the millinery shop to keep her brothers clothed and fed. She did a fine job by taking in boarders, but nobody except Uncle Henry ever said so. He's the one who slipped and told her that her father was living in Detroit under the unlikely name of Johanssen.

When she appeared on her father's front stoop and knocked on the door, he didn't have the foggiest who she was. He stood there in his undershirt with his trousers unbuckled, and he was wearing three days worth of whiskers. She primly removed her hat, straightened herself taller.

"Who are you and what in the hell do you want?" he asked.

Up the stairs a baby cried. A woman was singing to it.

With a knick-knack, paddy wack
Give a dog a bone
This old man came rolling home.

"Well?"

"Lilah," she announced. "Your daughter. Lilah?"

"Well, daughter Lilah, you be a good girl and hightail it out of here. Before I get nasty."

❖

The years went by; the babies dropped out of her, one after the other. But Lilah barely thought of anything except his leg, anyone but Artie. A loyal wife. When he clenched his fists she took to kissing the dips between each of his knuckles. She varnished his leg with cheesecloth and lemon oil, rubbing circles and circles around it the way she rubbed circles of oil around all her pregnant bellies, to avoid getting stretch marks.

One afternoon, when Artie gave off all the signs of being in a good and approachable mood, she nuzzled up to him and dared to say that she was the only woman who could have truly loved him. Loved him for who he was. She told him he had given her quite the life, which was close to the truth. She told him he was a looker, which was an outright lie.

"If you think I'm swanky, tell others," he said. "If you don't, just keep your trap shut."

"But I do! That's what I'm trying to tell you. All along, that's what I've been trying to say."

She was running off at the mouth now as far as he was concerned, making no sense at all. All this talk about love and sacrifice and being blessed, it made him want to puke in her wrinkled up old lap.

"In all my years," he said. "Never met anyone so friggin' useless."

"Oh, Artie, you know you don't mean that."

❖

When the other leg had to come off and Artie was forced to spend his days in bed, Lilah spoon-fed him his meals. He blubbered and snotted all over his pyjama top, begged her not to leave his side. He called her a saint, and that did it.

Oh, he grabbed her by the hair one Tuesday morning after he'd burned his tongue on the Quaker Oats, but he didn't follow through. He even apologized. Just like that, things weren't looking normal, no matter how hard she tried to convince herself they were. He was just not the man she married, the man who knew what was best for everybody, and assured her with his touch that she was alive.

By the time bedsores erupted on Artie's backside, Lilah had begun to hope he'd make a pass at one of the nurses who came by the house each week. The nurse could fall in love with him and take him off Lilah's hands. They could run away to Vegas and win a fortune at the one-armed bandits. Eat ladyfingers from their wedding cake. Take in that Elvis Presley fellow who could teach Artie a thing or two about wiggling your hips and getting women started.

The trouble was Artie liked to lift his loosened johnnycoat to give the girls a little thrill. Some nurses knew how to take him; others didn't. The ones that didn't would emerge quickly out of the bedroom, their faces flush with anger or embarrassment.

"Am I to take it you won't be coming back?" Lilah would say.

"How astute," the more assertive ones would respond.

"Artie's no prize, but then, who among us is?"

❖

As for Lilah, she is taking a breather while Artie languishes in Respite Care at Elizabeth-Bruyère Health Centre. She has repaired the fist and leg holes in the walls and while the plaster is drying, has headed down to pay her respects to her mother.

Sitting there by the starlit gladioli, she wonders what her life would be like if she had it to do all over.

"The same," she says to her mother. "I wouldn't change a blessed thing. Except maybe to give myself the name Marcia, and hair that didn't frizz in summer."

Under her breath she carefully mutters that Artie doesn't figure in the picture. That she'd still like to have a fling or two, a career as a hoofer on Broadway, and nowhere near the amount of children that she has.

"Aren't these flowers lovely, Mother? And no trouble whatsoever. As lovely as my life. A life as easy as pie for your oldest and your brightest. What a life I've had!"

Lilah tells herself, getting up with pins and needles in her legs, that eleven inches taller would be nothing to snub your nose at, that if she got herself fitted for one of those new-fangled prosthetic jobs, people couldn't keep themselves from looking up to her with awe, respect and envy. By the hour she could gaze at herself in that full length swivel dressing mirror. Never, never, never grow weary.

"If it's good enough for Artie," she could say, "then I'm sure it's good enough for me."

October Water

AFTER THE DREAM, I WADE INTO OCTOBER WATER AND WITHOUT clothes plunge into substance I can't see. There's a large area illuminated by moon and star, so I swim toward it briskly. This is because I'm afraid. I've read about swimmers getting pulled into an undertow and drowning. I've read about marathon swimmers on the Great Lakes who get eels wrapped around their legs. I'd die.

When I reach my circle of night light, I begin to tread water, guiding my arms and legs through currents of cold and colder. I could believe I am inside something safe if not for the ripples, the tremulous little waves that feel and look alive.

I race back for my heavy white robe by the shore and the smell of pine rising from the woodstove. I don't know what it is I'm hurrying to. Inside the cabin, the dream is waiting for me. It's a ritual: dream, swim, dream again. Every night I immerse myself in the lake, trying to avoid the dream. Avoiding it turns out to be impossible.

This cabin sits out of the way on a bluff. Inside, it's almost feral and eroding, though hints remain of a once cozy getaway trimmed with a woman's touch — baby animal knicknacks in front of the shelved books, dainty and fragile tea cups on the curio over in the corner, gilt-framed photographs of sunsets on the lake, plaid curtains identical to the tablecloth and lampshades, embroidered pillows on the rocking chair, porcelain windchimes hanging from a brass hook on the ceiling that sing as you brush past, that sometimes sing on their own.

The man who rented this place to me, Mr. Glynn, is a widower who's been living here year-round for too many years to remember exactly. The absence of humankind bothered him about as much as it bothers me and the water helped him sleep, he says, and kept him going. The ghost of his wife, Emily, would stand every day by the shore talking about their past and it was she, finally, who dove into the water one day, convincing him it was time to leave. He *has* left, but then again, he hasn't.

I've lived in this place for two months now. I cram so much thinking into one day that one day feels like a week. Feels like forever. I carry a lot of guilt for leaving my life behind like I did, but not enough to go back.

A squirrel, or some other rodent, scrabbles behind the kitchen walls, so I often shut the door and sit myself down in the livingroom, a patchwork quilt over my shoulders, to read a book of fairy tales I found nestled between some old magazines. *Cinderella. Hansel and Gretel. Tom Thumb.* I read them like a child who doesn't yet have access to sleeping pills, a child who has no need of them. As I read, I imagine the villains of my dreams pressing against the fragile panes of glass.

Sometimes, after reading, often with an old record on the Victrola, I accidentally nod off for a few minutes and fall into another dream. They're all different, but they're all the same dream too. I know that much. It hardly matters though. Some stories you remember and the ones you forget stalk you like obsessive lovers.

Waking, I hear the squirrel between the walls, the record looping round and round; my mother.

❖

My mother, in the dream, is standing stiff and upright on a black square of a black and white checkered floor. Her breathing, hurried and desperate, is what tugs me awake every time. Reproaches rise in my throat and make me feel like screaming. They press against the walls of my head, making me want to yank out my hair and toss clumps of it into the fire instead of pine cones. WHY DON'T YOU MOVE? WHY DON'T YOU DO SOMETHING? I want to hear some other sound besides the sound of my mother's breathing. The sound of movement would be a comfort, her limbs swishing against the fabric of her clothes.

What stops me from screaming, even in the dream, I don't know. Then I think, civility, that's what, the civility of an only child who should be thankful she hasn't been spoiled. But is that it? Or is it the waves outside lapping against the shore in some interminable, nauseating foreplay, trying to get my attention like men back in the city? These waves annoy me. I've come here to listen to nothing; to be reminded of nothing; to get away.

The water is black with a mercurial silver on its surface. It looks the same at night as it does during the day, and the wind, when I get to it, always feels the same against my skin — gentle and cool. I stand naked before the water as though it were a lover who must assess the beauty of my body before accepting me. A ceremony. What if someone were to see? I'm not very demure, I think. Far from it.

Mr. Glynn finds reasons to be here. He brings me food from town, comes to chop wood and to weed a garden he knows I don't know how to care for. He is spared the shock of seeing how I have changed the furniture around, refusing, as he does, to come inside. He told me on the day I signed the lease that he liked Emily's things *just so*.

If we have tea, we have it standing by the car. If I make him biscuits or muffins and invite him to eat these inside by the fire, he says some other time. Often he gets on to how much he regrets seeing me here, a woman alone in the bush on a lake not big enough to drown in. Someone with my looks, don't I have a fellow? He calls men *fellows*. I tell him about all my boyfriends and how I never fail to leave them, when I leave them, with the impression that things are their fault.

Mr. Glynn tells me I'm hopeless. You're hopeless, he says, would you just look at those weeds. Say, for a minute, I *am* hopeless and say, for a minute, I could change that. I could change that if you like, I say, and brush my lips down the side of his neck, run my tongue over his Adam's apple. Mr. Glynn pushes me away, chastening me that he's old enough to be my father.

❖

In the dream my mother is forever asking where my father is. Why isn't he in this with me, she asks, her tone causing her already grim features to harshen. Why doesn't he have to be here?

It begins with my mother sneaking a cigarette, furtively stealing puffs while I remain hidden away in a closet, watching her through a crack. She thinks nobody knows what she's up to, but her fits of coughing and the haze of staleness around our house are a dead giveaway. In the way spies are, I am suspicious. I'm hoping to catch her.

My mother is tall and slender. Though the boiling water in front of her on the stove practically spills over, she doesn't stop stirring. Her slippered right foot sweeps a mound of breadcrumbs under the oven. Sweeps and sweeps, annoyed by the unsightly breadcrumbs. She comes closer to me, pulls the door open.

A-ha! she yells. Yanks me out, to ask if my father is present. I've looked for him. I can't find him.

Look harder, she says and blows smoke rings that drift above us to the ceiling.

Suddenly my father shouts at my mother from the top of the stairs. I can see he is naked and that he holds a leather strap in his hand. His face is darkness. She has two minutes, my mother, to get upstairs. A minute and a half. Thirty seconds.

With scissors I travel through the Sears Home Furnishings Catalogue, cutting out tables, chairs, couches, lamps. And then I paste them to a white page. My clean house has walls of pristine white. Priscilla-style curtains frame the view of the starkest, bluest sky I've ever seen. A door slams and I cut around a canopy bed and glue it snugly between two night tables.

❖

It's not like a name that's on the tip of your tongue, I would tell my mother if she were here. There's nobody to ask; there's no trick. I can't, for instance, pour through the letters of the alphabet, trying to jog my memory. There's nothing to do except wait. I can't remember his face and that's all there is to it.

I remember his arms, all puffed up, the definition of his muscles. Come and see the way his jackets hang so neatly in his closet. Blacks, then browns, then the camel hair, the green, the blues, the maroon. Come watch the way he polishes his shoes, then places them in ruler straight rows. Notice how he dresses: shirt, socks, first right foot, then left, pants, tie, belt, jacket, a quick glance in the mirror as he runs a comb through the Brylcreem in his hair. When he does his push-ups, count with him to one hundred in his even tone between even, regular breaths. Taste the food he eats: three shakes of salt, two of pepper, the meat, the vegetables, the bread, his rye in one crowning gulp.

Seventeen years is a long time. My father walked out on us seventeen years ago. Mr. Man, my mother used to call him behind his back. King of the wooden hill.

I came home from school one day, soaking wet from walking in the rain. My mother was sweeping the kitchen floor. The radio was turned way up, the dial set slightly off the station. She didn't seem to mind the static interfering with Glen Campbell singing "Honey, Come Back". I was in love with Glen Campbell at the time. I was in love with a lot of men on the radio.

Her sweeping looked like ballroom dancing, the broom like a partner she was leading. Our kitchen floor was checkered black and white, polished to a dangerous perfection. She was frumpy, not dressed the way she took to dressing after he left. The way she moved suggested she had acres around her, she had air and sky and water to dance on.

The night before, my father sat me on the dog's bowl in the corner. He forced my mother to kneel, naked, inside a square, one foot by one foot. With his strong arms flexed, he stood there, taunting. He forbade my mother to move, even to whimper and then pulled her head back and slammed it forward, commanding her not to miss one drop.

She did and he made her lick it off the floor.

In the silver of the toaster I can see my mother's purple face. I catch my mother's purple face in the toaster as she dances, although it's never reflected long enough for me to see the contours of her open mouth, the shape of her teeth. I am forced to imagine whitish liquid spilling thickly out the sides, sliding down her body. She's polishing the floor with it because she wants to. That's why the floor is so shiny, not because he makes her keep it that way.

Normally, by the time I came home from school on days like this, you could expect to find my mother rearranging flowers, crying quietly over a poem in which my father was begging forgiveness and promising reform. That's what I had been expecting to find when I walked in the door and placed my books on the cedar chest in the front hall. My mother would tell me that my father was going back on the wagon, that he was going to be treating us to another family celebration at some expensive restaurant.

But what she tells me is that his car is found abandoned on Mackenzie King's summer estate in the Gatineau where, before they were married or even engaged, I was conceived.

Nobody offers to explain the disappearance of his clothes, his luggage, the withdrawal of funds from the bank account. My mother is thankful that the commerce of everyone else's ideas is taking place without her. She shoves his wedding ring down the drain instead of his liquor.

❖

Sometimes the dream goes this far. A man behind me has placed a hand on my shoulder. His grip hurts. I know who it is, but I'm not about to look into his face. I am being held down between two big legs in a bathtub that is deep for a little body. I'm at the bottom of an ocean, I think. Deeper.

The window affords me the steady view of clouds that look like intestines made of smoke, an unreachable sky. I'm cleaving to the edge of the bathtub and I know my knuckles are white and bony although they're not what I look at. There is nothing I want to watch except sky. The clouds. They drift by and beyond the perfect geometry of the window and prove to me that the world is round and that it does turn, just like Mrs. Bertrand taught us.

The floorboards just outside the bathroom door creak under the weight of my mother's footfall. She says, walking by, that the sound of splashing suits my pretty little face. And then sound disappears just like the clouds all clumped together, all twisted and tangled, clouds that tighten for a second and then discharge into delicate, airy fragments.

I spot a castle. A fairy in a beautiful dress, her magic wand at the ready. A house made of candy floss. I'm on a street corner, on somebody's shoulders, way up high. I'm watching a parade on Bank Street and I can see my breath when I exhale, getting away from me, wispy and determined as a cloud.

So it is not my mother's breathing which tugs me awake when I dream this one, but my own. It is the sound also of Emily's windchimes. The sound of the rocking chair rocking and creaking on its own. The up and down of it making me sick.

I move the chair from place to place, trying to make it stop, but it never does. It goes on and on, rocking full tilt. I can almost see my father in it. A wizened, balding man with a touch of white hair, a tooth missing from his bottom plate. A man who would wobble if he were to get up and walk. A man who would weep for his incontinence. Who would weep for no reason at all.

I can almost see myself in the chair, a young child enfolded in my mother's arms. Thumb in mouth, I am memorizing my mother's face, allowing my muscles to go limp, surrendering to the heaviness of my eyelids. At this age, I trust sleep. Sleep is not a trick at this age, or a punishment.

But the sounds persist, inside and outside. They grow louder and chase me out into the lake.

When I emerge from my swim, dizzy from breathing poorly and not getting far enough, my skin on fire despite the coldness, I run into Mr. Glynn. Evidently he's got nothing better to do and it's a human touch I'm craving. Come inside, I say.

But he refuses the way he has all the times before, looking away from me out on the water. I realize he plans to go on refusing until Emily steps out of the lake to join him, the silver of the lake rippling all over her body.

Nothing has happened for so long, I can almost believe that time is coming. Their arms linked, they will walk into the cabin together and I will follow close behind. I'll sit myself in the chair. Or lie down on the couch. Or I'll wrap myself in the quilt and lie down on the floor. It won't matter, because Mr. Glynn and Emily will be standing there, watching over me. For the first time I will fall asleep without wondering if I can.

In the Time
It Takes to Breathe

"Ms. Barton-Hill, here, grew up when she was eight."
My relatives still say that about me. They think it's funny. Sometimes I do too. They attribute my sudden maturity to the fact I lost a spelling bee to a third grade girl who'd cheated. In fact I grew up in the time it took to breathe, just before my father's breakdown and just after he convinced me I was going to die one day and I'd better live quickly.

This is how I put it together:

My father strolled with his arm in mine from kitchen to bedroom. He stood me up against the wall, parted my bangs lovingly the way he always did when they needed to be cut. He took aim at me with his rifle, one eye closed. He inserted the barrel in my mouth, shoved it to the back of my throat, pulled the trigger. The taste of metal mixed with the taste of nosebleed. On the wall, painted a vanilla, not quite white, not quite yellow, I rubbed my fingers raw.

He snapped his fingers, saying, "One minute here, the next minute, gone."

While he was having electric shock treatments and learning to play bridge with three other men in pyjamas, I lost count of the people who asked me what I was going to be when I grew up.

Sick of the question, sick of my own voice, I would answer defiantly, "A teacher. Maybe a history teacher, just like my dad."

❖

Beyond a momentary note of good looks or good body, I never thought I'd have much to do with men. At nineteen, going on twenty, I ended up marrying the boy next door. It was a very adult thing to do; I still think that. He could cook, type, and tell me he loved me, in words. I love you was something he said to me every day, once in the morning, once at night. Always worried about the eczema on my hands flaring up without a moment's notice, he did dishes as well.

An uncle, my mother's brother, my father's replacement, gave me away. His firm grip kept me steady, upright, as we made our way down the long aisle. The whole thing flew by me and all I remember is the reception line, people offering me congratulations on the ceremony, the hall, the preparations.

My uncle told them all, "Ms. Barton-Hill is the planner in the family. She's already planned her own funeral."

Ten minutes away, my father was strapped to a bed with tears in his eyes and drool on his chin. He was in a panic, rambling on and on, because I was about to be imprisoned in an illusion of stability.

"There are too many people in the world! Too many books! So much happening and no time to learn from it."

He couldn't remember anything of his childhood. His memory had been erased. They had wiped everything away except what they should have: the hearse carrying his father's murdered body, boring a hole through the freezing rain. And the rage, my father's rage at the traffic which, as a boy, he had watched become courteous and gentle and slow.

The photographer kept us on our feet until dinner was served. In the pictures I am the centre of attention, the focus in my long virginal dress. The dress protected what I'd given away on an impulse many years before, just to get it over with. Long satin gloves covered my hands which were covered themselves with a thick, red crust.

❖

In three seconds flat, at age thirty-three, I fell in love for the first time. It wasn't with my husband. A cameraman, along with a reporter from the CBC, came into my classroom to shoot a segment of my lecture "Romance: The Myth and its Makers".

He offered his hand; I gave him my name. "A name with a hyphen always gets my attention," he said.

When he placed the microphone on my chest, he grazed my nipple. There might be such things as accidents; but I didn't think so. Moving about the amphitheatre, up and down the steps, between the students and the tables with that bulk of camera slung over his shoulder, he would lower his body and raise it. He would advance to the podium where I stood, and retreat, making sure he was noticed. He didn't have to try so hard, though; I couldn't have missed him. His presence was something I could practically taste.

"You look lovely," he mouthed.

In one second, everything I had taught myself about men flew out the window. I had been waiting for him all of my life! Everything in my life had been building to this moment! It seemed larger than life alright and I had better hurry and make connections from one word to another, from one thing to the next. From the newscast the following day I could see my eyes glowed, belladonna wide, looking for him behind the camera. Tall, dark-haired, bearded, and older. Nothing, as they say, like the sun. Nothing like any ideal man I could construct in one of my fantasies. Nothing I could put my finger on, at the time.

He gathered wires with such confidence I instantly had faith he would know just what to do in the bedroom. It was as though the words "feminism", "freedom" rolled off someone else's tongue as mine disengaged from a dance with his. He undid my blouse. With one hand he unhooked my bra. He put the nipple he had grazed in his mouth. And there, in the background of the classroom, were my students with raised hands and questions already blocked out for them so they wouldn't have to think.

Devoutly he traced the bones in my face and the fullness of my lips. One of my students said, "I find that point very interesting."

He ran his hands over my body, reached up under my skirt and feeling wetness there, filled me with his fingers, his knee. We made love standing up, my hips rising and falling. The rasp of paint on bare skin echoed and I heard some smart ass yell, "I don't think so!"

When I came, it felt as though I would slip down a tunnel

inside myself, down my own throat. If I didn't cling to his shoulders I *would* disappear. I only realized I was still alive when my back scraped its way down the wall. Relieved, I fell to my knees. I took him in my mouth and God, he tasted sweet.

I finished up my lecture by saying, "So it's no wonder the idea of a man gets created in his absence. He doesn't communicate. That's how he gets entangled in a woman's dream, fantasy, her obsession."

And it was with a certain happy, flaunting drama that I took an ordinary sip of water from my cup as the cameraman contemplated me from behind the camera when there was nothing left to shoot.

❖

In a segment of the next day's news, a Walton-sized family sat around a slab of table. At the head, the father amiably chided one of his sons for a boarding house reach. A dinner roll was tossed. Crumbs fell from my husband's sandwich. We were lying in bed. The crumbs swirled like snowflakes in a light wind over the plate in his lap. He daubed his middle finger to his tongue and picked them up. That could have been his family there, he said. Some eight kids, a father carving roast, a mother pouring gravy, a room abuzz with conversation.

He must have sensed something was up with me. It wasn't like him to brag.

When he chewed, his right jaw clicked and saliva sloshed around in his mouth. I upped the volume on the remote so Iraqi soldiers could stride toward him. So their bullets wouldn't crackle in the background like mere popcorn. Bullets were real.

It was just my husband had never had to learn to believe it.

"You want news?" I said.

I told him about the cameraman, how my body was turning inside out. I rubbed cortisone cream into the cracks on my hands. The cream filled the spaces in my wedding ring and dulled the diamonds.

"You'll be seeing some of his work," I said.

"Not in this lifetime," he said, and the television went dead. "And just so you know, excitement will fizzle out before you can spell it." He hesitated, then added, "If that's what you're looking for."

Apparently there were a lot of needy people in this city. Fifteen cars, my husband had counted, in a motel parking lot at noon. His boss and his boss's secretary both came back late. My father had called, needed money. My mother had called to see if my father had called. My father's new wife too, to let me know my father was riding the buses again with a Luger strapped to his ankle.

"Needy people abound, as you can see."

"And I am one of them. Is that what you're saying?" I asked.

It may have been what he was saying, but he wasn't about to say anymore. He threw a few things in a bag and left the room. Downstairs, the lock on the front door clicked. I heard my husband's footsteps along the walkway, the garage door opening, the engine turning over, the car driving away.

My head, resting on my pillow, rested on the cameraman's shoulder. He had said I might be too young for him. On the other hand, I might be too old. The reporter told me the cameraman was already involved with someone half his age. When the cameraman passed me his business card it felt like a baton in a relay. He said you never knew, he might take one of my classes some day. He said he had a lot to learn about love.

Over our first drink he proceeded down the long list of his

inconsolable losses. He neither looked at me nor took a breath between the words. My skin was driving me insane. I wanted to scratch until I bled. My mouth was on fire, but he continued to talk in his softly effusive voice while an urge to kiss him ate away at my lips.

I let his scent fill my body. I let the taste of him make me dizzy until, finally, his mouth was on mine.

Considering what I was about to lose, a kiss was such a small thing to want. I felt entitled to it.

❖

As it turned out, my husband left me and never returned. For two of the three years I was with the cameraman my skin was as white as my wedding dress. On the day I figured out sex with him wasn't what I thought it was, I calculated my father owed me forty thousand dollars — one thousand dollars, not including interest, for every year I'd been alive. For making it impossible for anyone to compete with him, or take his place.

This, I suppose, is how I really put us all together:

At age it-doesn't-matter-because-it-happened-so-many-times I sat on the curb at the end of our street, waiting for my father to come home from work. He had an important meeting with his floozie from the School Board and my mother guessed if he didn't forget his way home he'd arrive about half past eight.

The chip wagon parked in front of our house spewed the smell of grease, making my mouth water and stomach growl. I would rather starve, however, than eat without my father.

Except for a boy leaning up against the brick, the schoolyard across from me was empty. The kid shuffled his feet, kicked up sand. I wondered if he was in my father's class and if he knew his history the way I did.

The last of my pebbles splashed into the sewer beneath my feet. My father sluggishly rounded the corner, his heavy jacket flung over his shoulder. A box of Cracker Jacks was for me. I ran to him, placed my feet on his feet, wound my arms around his waist and we walked like this along the side of the house, up the fire escape at the back, up two long flights.

"It's a kazillion degrees out here," he said, sitting on the top rail, smiling his superior teacher's smile. "Your daddy needs his head examined."

He edged his body outward and let his back fall and slam against the metal. He gripped the rail with the backs of his knees. With a handkerchief he mopped the sweat from his face. His eyes were bloodshot and swollen. Two perspiration stains discoloured his shirt under the armpits. I noticed this just after he shot the ground with his finger.

"I could fall," he warned. "I could fall and crack my skull open on the cement down there."

Way up in the sky the sun was dull white with a ribbon of cloud through its middle. It looked like an Easter egg and Easter was coming. I hugged my father's feet. I hugged them so tight with my raw red hands. Don't look down, you stupid stupid.

I knew where he had to look. But it wasn't my place to tell him.

Celestial Names

NOW THAT SHE TAKES A GOOD LOOK, CORINNE'S NOT SURE she's wearing the right thing at all. A tent of a dress, all turquoise sky with navy mountains, three broad strokes of chalk across the front and a lone black bird, soaring from breast to breast. No matter which way she tilts her head the bird looks like a blob of tar flung by one of her kids years ago to tell her something she needed to know. It catches her eye over and over, and over and over she gets sucked into trying to dust it off like something that's not supposed to be there.

Her eyes are lovely, quite lovely, blue and green at once, the colour of her dress. But who the hell is going to notice her eyes? This man, this Theodore Johnson from the personals? Corinne is not talking to herself, but to *Donahue*, which she doesn't have time for today. Annette in the next room is watching the same thing with the volume turned higher.

Girls in gangs. Rolling the dice to see how many guys you'd

have to bag in bed to be initiated. Drive-by shootings, tagging your name on the walls of your 'hood. She'll get Annette to tell her about it later, although Annette, given half a chance, could talk your face off, or into something.

In front of Corinne is a bowl of popcorn dowsed in soya sauce, a bag of ju-jubes and the newspaper opened to the RSVP section. Four or five ads are outlined in *Rouge Bonjour Soufflé* lipstick Annette has transferred from her lips to the print. That's Annette. Very dramatic. Annette's not even her real name; it's the name she's going by at the moment as she studies to become a better actress than the one she used to be, before she knew it was a discipline she could master.

The girls on TV, in contrast to Corinne, are wearing leather jackets and bandannas around their heads. Their consciences have been eroded, Corinne can tell, by the people and the systems that have failed them. She stares at them the same way she stares at people who snap gum, wear sunglasses, sing along with their car radios as they drive by. She stares with the kind of amazement that may as well be envy.

Corinne would like to be a guest on Phil's show and tell him about how she hasn't moved a muscle since the day Henry left, reminding her it was because she was too fat. That was almost twenty years ago. On his way out the door he said nobody would ever give her a second look, but she's fooled him on that score. One look isn't enough to take her in anymore.

"Phil," she'd say, "I knew I'd make him eat those words if it was the last thing I ever did."

She would confess that Henry had left her on the same day the nutritionist at Figure Magic weighed her in at only twenty pounds shy of her ideal weight. When Corinne told Henry the good news, he stared and asked how she felt about producing a brain-damaged child. There was a big clump of hamburger hanging from his mouth.

Corinne would tell Phil that Henry then recommended she pick up a girdle the next time she was at Miracle Mart. She was still wearing her jogging pants with her body suit which clung to the sweat on her skin. Her cleavage, a thin black line between two pendulous fruits, what her mother referred to as Eve's pocket, made her wince and she reached for a towel to cover herself.

By then Henry was impotent, impotent with *her* that was. Henry blamed this on Scotty whom he called the mental retard, although Corinne knew Henry's problem began after Jennifer, their first, was born.

"He got up and said he wanted a divorce, and it was just like that. My mother-in-law Mildred showed up the next day to get the meat grinder she gave us as a wedding gift and my mother came to tell Mildred to tell Henry I apologized. My mother expressed some concern I wouldn't be able to take care of myself, what with the three children, and Scotty. All Mildred had to say to her was, 'I don't want to be a crepehanger, but let's face it, Camilla.'

"My doctor said it was the Madonna-Whore complex. 'That's what I have?' I asked. His doctor said it was psychosomatic. Henry said, 'Baloney!' And then he started to down his Valium with Cinzano, to nick his face while shaving, to be home later and later, and less and less often. His mother seemed to enjoy pointing out that he was taking along his secretary to sales conventions."

❖

Corinne's hair has been swept to the top of her head in an obsolescence of bubbles which Annette takes pride in calling a bold fashion statement. The lipstick, Annette's, is too red for her thin lips and she rummages through the clutter of Root Beer cans on her bureau until she finds a scarf to wipe it off.

She removes a Mr. Big from her stash in the drawer, tears the wrapper with as careful a touch as she used to apply the turquoise to her eyelids. She doesn't bite the chocolate, but sucks and savours it, lets it linger between the roof of her mouth and the floor of her tongue the way her mother told her she must do with the body of Christ at communion.

During thunderstorms, Corinne still sprinkles holy water in every room, imitating her mother who is afraid of the apocalypse. The end of the world as Corinne knows it is something Corinne is secretly looking forward to. The sound of trumpets. Henry being roughed up by the wind, pelted with hail, splattered with blood. And her, like an angel, lending a hand.

She's never, come to think of it, engaged in an act of defiance. Her divorce would have been the first but her mother had raised such a stink that Corinne had coughed up the money for an annulment. For her mother's sake she had allowed herself to be subjected to probing questions on the nature of her sex life from someone who had taken a lifelong vow of celibacy. From someone who probably poked his pecker into little boys' behinds when nobody was looking.

Corinne smells her armpits, then dips the scarf in holy water and applies it like deodorant. She scrubs at the red around her mouth, the smudge of chocolate on her front tooth.

The girls on Phil's stage have been joined by a rival gangmember. Her attitude, petulant and contrary, brings out a hostility in the audience Corinne always finds entertaining. Each of the girls stands up in turn and spraypaints her name on a wall. They are celestial names, not the names given to them by their mothers: Moon, Jupiter, Paradise. They are careful not to touch each other's names, deface the scrawls.

They're still just like young girls, Corinne thinks: careful to keep their printing on the lines, careful not to scribble outside the borders of their colouring books.

But the audience would like some scribbling, would like one fleck of paint to land on another just to see what would happen, what little provocation it would take to make tempers flare. Phil, if he'd thought of it, might have provided an even smaller wall — it would have been good for the ratings. Instead he is trying to feed them the sanctity of life and self-reliance, as though both were brussels sprouts or anchovies for which a taste can be acquired.

As she feeds herself popcorn she wonders what there will be to eat at the restaurant. Theodore Johnson is going to treat her to an all-you-can-eat buffet, but she's not sure what that means. She's not sure about Theodore Johnson either.

MATURE MALE RECENTLY WIDOWED SEEKS MATURE FEMALE LONG DIVORCED. That's what the ad had said.

Annette figures Corinne has reached a predictable crisis for a woman her age and weight: "You're fifty-three years old and it's time you got cracking." Before it's too late Corinne should have a companion drawn to the cushions of her flesh, to the scent of lemon bath splash tucked into her creases, masking the odour of stale powder. You couldn't live with men, but then you had to face the fact you couldn't live without them either. "It's no picnic being alone. Corinne, you know that."

Men who like fat women exist; Phil's had them on his show. Men with fat woman fantasies, fat woman fetishes. Men who knead rolls of flesh with greasy hands, men who lather fat ladies with Crisco shortening. It might make Henry jealous. It might make the kids stand up and take notice. And there was Annette to consider, Annette who's been entertaining the notion of moving out West if something in her life doesn't change soon. Corinne hardly likes to think of herself in this house without her, without Annette rehearsing Hamlet's "To

Be Or Not To Be" at all hours of the night. The way things are, the way they have been for the last two years since Scotty moved into the group home, Annette's annoyed her so much, Corinne hasn't had time to be lonely.

"Phil, I tried to tell her that choosing men from an ad is belittling. No different than the guests on your show choosing Filipino brides from a mail-order catalogue."

Annette reminded her she wouldn't have to marry the guy, just check him out. "For me," she'd added with a very pronounced pout which didn't work and then a bout of silence and sulking which did.

"Have you ever?" she'd asked Annette.

"Once."

"Once?"

"Once."

"And?"

"And that won't happen to you." This Annette had said with a dismissive flourish of the feather duster. This season she was playing the part of a maid who pretends she's French from France in order to get special attention and privileges.

Corinne and Annette had been having one of their no-men-allowed pyjama parties. Corinne was content to just lie back and listen to Annette dish the dirt about members of the cast. The steady climb of her voice affected Corinne in the same way as Oreo cookies; it sated her hunger and calmed her.

Annette had told her the widower didn't give a flying fig about looks. "Corinne, you're in like Flinn."

She had related to Corinne several times already, in slightly different versions, the period in her life when she had been obsessed with a man — married, unavailable, a critic and a celebrity of sorts. She would sit by the phone hour after hour, day after day, fly every time it rang, which it almost never did. Corinne knew she was still waiting, acting as if she wasn't.

"You have to take the initiative sooner or later, that's exactly what you have to do."

"What does *he* look like? Does it say?" Corinne had asked.

"Nobody pukes when he walks into a room, but nobody notices him either." Annette snapped back the newspaper and buried her face in it.

"You're making that up."

"Am not."

Corinne could never tell when Annette was lying. She had scrutinized her as though it might help, though it never had before. One of her arms was bigger than Annette's waist. One of her legs weighed more than all of Annette put together. An ear of mine, she had thought, wouldn't fit into that mouth of hers. And yet lies the size of watermelons fell from those scarlet lips every day. Annette got tangled up in her lies. They were the only things that kept her from vanishing into thin air.

"He could look like Phil, you never know," she said suddenly, trying to push Corinne into the nineties.

Corinne had to admit it. She liked the look of Phil, always had, the way he ran up and down aisles with his coattails swinging from side to side, the way he was not too vain to appear before a camera with wisps of hair sticking up from behind his head. She remembered him from his early days when he had sideburns and saucy women on his show. Twenty-five years on the air had to tell you something. Henry used to call him a besotted liberal and warned her she could get just as fat on his ideas as she could on truffles and the Pop Shoppe.

"Some men like fat women, I hear. But you'll have to tell him first I'm fat."

"Gargantuan."

"He's probably just the opposite. Skin and bones."

"I'll get you dolled up. He won't know what hit him."

"You do that."

Annette had added that she thought he had a great sense of humour. "Oh I love it when they can tell jokes and do all the accents!"

"The last thing I want, Phil, is a comedian. At my tenth anniversary party Henry told a joke that went over real big. I can never remember the build-up, but the punch line is unforgettable. Henry said, 'Take this morning. I'm meaning to ask Corinne to pass me the butter and instead I say you're ruining my fucking life, bitch.'"

But she hadn't said any of this to Annette. She just lay there, listening.

Meanwhile, Annette was splitting a gut over a review of her play, the reference to the leading lady's command of the stage. At first her laughter was genuine, but it quickly became self-conscious, imitative of some actress she'd seen in the movies.

"You be Ingrid, the private detective with a heavy caseload," she said. "I'll be your secretary and call him. Make all the arrangements for you." She bowed her torso, cracked her long, tapered fingers.

Annette was not just skinny, but anorexic. Corinne considered this might have something to do with the fact Annette was still in her twenties, or with the fact she hadn't had children. Maybe something to do with that man who still lived inside her, devouring her innards, slaking his thirst on the very juice in her bones. Annette was awaiting a response, complicity.

"If my name's Ingrid, who are you?" obliged Corinne. Annette giggled and kicked the furry slippers from her feet.

"I know, I know. I'll be your body guard!"

Together they chopped the mattress into a thousand pieces with their hands. "Karate," Annette told her and flung herself back, content to watch all this drama unfold in front of her.

"Oh God, I haven't dated a man since Buddy D'Orazio and he was a boy." Corinne placed a hand on Annette's bony wrist, squeezed.

"You never forget," said Annette. "It's like riding a bike. Just siddown and start pedalling. If you don't pedal, you won't move."

The two of them on their backs started to pedal in the air, Annette first and Annette faster.

"Phil, you had to be there. My bare, bulky, dimpled legs, sticking out of my nightgown. They looked more like heels and toes fending off air, an upside down Highland Fling."

Corinne hadn't been able to keep it up and, breathless, allowed her legs to fall. Her legs bounced a few times, shaking the bed. The springs creaked and both women let out groans of pleasure. Corinne was thinking of Dempster's Bakery, craving the smell of fresh bread you can't help but catch when you drive by on the Queensway, up one ramp and down the other, eastbound, westbound.

"In my mind, I have to tell you, Phil, I was dipping the bread in sugared milk and feeding it to Annette. She was still pedalling away. Didn't even realize she was hungry."

It's almost ten o'clock and a man's voice is asking whether she wants a transcript of the show. Corinne jots the address down and notices she has soya sauce imbedded under her fingernails, popcorn stuck between her teeth. She can hear the television in Annette's room and Annette rooting around the bathroom downstairs.

"Throw me up the floss."

"Are you just about ready? We haven't got all day."

Corinne blows herself a kiss after she draws thick, heart-shaped lips over her reflection in the mirror, and pokes a black beauty mark on its chin.

Annette sticks her head in and assures her, in case Corinne's having second thoughts, that it's way too late to back out now. She advances toward the television and turns it off. She adjusts Corinne's dress so her bra straps aren't showing, grabs her purse, shoves her out the door, down the stairs, outside, and loads her into the van. They have trouble with the seat belt again and Annette promises to pay the fine if they're stopped.

Corinne warns that her nerves have brought on diarrhoea and she is told to hold it. Annette will drive really, really fast, and pay the fine for that, too.

❖

At the restaurant, a head of ham is crowned with pineapple, thorns of cherries and cloves. Salads, rice, a whole trolley of Napoleons and eclairs over to the left. A man with a tubular white hat pours Grand Marnier on Corinne's four pieces of French toast and sets it on fire. Whipped cream. A blood river of berries. Corinne comes away with two plates, returns for juice and black coffee.

"A woman with an appetite," Annette remarks, "I like that."

Since Theo's a no-show, Annette takes it upon herself to remark on the colour of Corinne's dress, how it sets off her eyes, on the bird over her breasts, so eye-catching, how she has never failed to notice how jolly some fat people can be.

For the life of her Corinne cannot understand why she doesn't feel insulted for being stood up. Unless it has something to do with the fact Annette warned her it might happen, that, or there mightn't be any chemistry. All she knows is she feels safe here with the tops of her thighs crushed against the table's underside, brave for having squeezed into this tight-fitting space.

Annette pecks at her food; Corinne gorges herself. Annette is a Pisces; Corinne is a Virgo. Annette is thinking of becoming a lesbian; Corinne is quite sure she'll remain celibate. Annette believes in reincarnation; Corinne would like to, but thinks it's against her religion. Annette believes in living with a person a long, long time before you marry them; Corinne tells Annette about her recurring dream of the apocalypse. Annette places her hands together in prayer and claims that opposites attract.

Corinne catches her reflection in the mirror at the bar. One of her bubbles is drooping. The bird on her chest stops her heart momentarily because she thinks she has sloppily spilled sauce from the ribs. And here is Annette, so beautiful, the waiters are falling over themselves to serve her. Annette calls them parasites when they manage to tear away from the table. "The parasites," she says. When she says this, she inserts a finger to the back of her throat in a mock gesture of vomiting.

Something in the gesture makes Corinne want to vomit herself, and she blurts out, "You need to see a doctor."

Corinne hunkers down to retrieve a dropped spoon and takes notice of Annette's skinny ankles. Without thinking she taps the spoon on Annette's knee cap and when it doesn't kick out reflexively she does it again. And then again on the other. Her stomach tightens.

"I have to go to the washroom."

When together they arrive in the washroom Corinne points to her zipper; she needs Annette to help her remove her unsuitable dress and Annette does so, scouting for a stain. As Annette gathers two bunches of hem at the sides and lifts them over Corinne's head, Corinne notices that the washroom is empty, that the faucets are covered in soap scum, the sinks are heaped with dry paper towels. A bulging caterpillar slinks over the baseboard. What a mess, she thinks. If the world's not running away, it's running down.

Corinne's two arms go high above, but fall to shoulder height. She spreads them outward when standing there in her bra and panties, her sensible shoes.

"I need air," she says. "I need all the air in this world to keep from falling unconscious. I knew I shouldn't have come. It's like my whole life is happening again and it was bad enough the first time."

Corinne closes her eyes and reads her skin by touch, the softness, the hardness, the lumps, the ridges. Behind her eyes she sees white. The white light of the sinks and toilets, the white of her bra and panties, her naked skin, the white of her skin, drained of blood.

"This is what it must feel like to be an angel," she says to Phil. "You can float or fly, walk through a wall and disappear, hover above the world on a cloud, stand on a mountaintop and yell into the air. The yelling is the thing, isn't it, and the waiting to see what comes back."

Corinne directs herself to a toilet seat and plops herself down. Then she stands, lowers her panties, sits down again and begins to pee. The liquid gushes and gushes.

"Have you flipped? Somebody's gonna charge in here and see," says Annette.

Annette walks over, pulls the stall door closed and stands there, holding it. "Do you know what my mother told me? That you couldn't pee with a tampon in."

"My mother thinks tampons are a sin. And that advertising them on television is scandalous. She's written letters, even tried to get petitions going. You won't believe this, but she's even tried to finagle her way onto Phil's show."

On both sides of her and in front, the stall is full of names, limericks, phone numbers and laments. The etchings are all metallic looking, greyish silvery letters and numbers surfacing from carved-away paint. Keys and coins, she thinks. There is a surge of something like electricity fanning out from her heart and she wonders if this is another impulse that will betray her.

"Annette, come and write your name in red lipstick, like those girls from the show this morning. Let's do something."

Annette lets the door swing open, begins to scrutinize the graffiti. She inserts a finger to the back of her throat, presumably because most of the advertisement is about unrequited love. Then Annette takes out her lipstick and, hoarding the space of the whole wall over the toilet paper dispenser, writes STAR and frames it with one.

Corinne wipes herself, hikes up her panties, notices Annette's bony wrists, smudged with red. She plucks the lipstick from Annette's hand. "It just occurred to me," she says, "that I will never be thin and that you will never be fat. I'm a little slow to catch on to things; that never occurred to me before."

On the opposite wall, she writes ANGEL and over it, FOR A GOOD TIME CALL.

If she were going to go all the way, she'd have to confess to Phil that Angel was the name of Henry's secretary. Corinne never met her or asked what she looked like, just pictured her as a white-robed thing with a halo shining brightly over her head as she spread her legs open for Henry's pleasure, which she could sustain eternally. Henry said Angel didn't mean a blessed thing and after he left Corinne, didn't move in with Angel to prove it. Mildred said Angel had been a godsend in her son's difficult life. Corinne's mother said that people these days had to strive to be more forgiving.

"We should put our real names, I suppose," she says to Annette. "If we don't put our real names, I don't think it counts."

"I'll do you one better," says Annette and she draws a red devil, with horns and pitchfork. "Go to Hell, Theodore Johnson!" she writes.

Corinne takes the lipstick back and gives the devil a mustache and a goatee like Henry's. Beside him she draws a thin, sexy angel with ample breasts and huge, red nipples. She's careful to give Henry a limp penis, not too big, eyes that droop and a frown. Bold, blood-red flames shoot out from both bodies, become bigger and bolder until the lipstick breaks from the tube. It lands at Corinne's feet, hot and heavy from her zeal.

Like A Bride's Nightie

MURIEL CONCENTRATES ON THE LAND AROUND HER, A DULL-looking field, yellowed after snowmelt, stinking like rot, like death. Weeping willows hunch over, corroded with a spent and dying winter. The wind slams into her face as though trying to enter her body by the mouth. The wind is determined. She has given up the idea that the bird waltzing above her in the air is Howard. Even so, this is where she came to find him, in the middle of nothing, and nowhere, behind the house where they danced together for the last fifty-one years.

If she kept walking, she would come, eventually, to the edge of the square earth. Muriel sees herself as an explorer and life in terms of the land. You claim a part of it, shunt back and forth, covering it with the signature of your body and when there's no more land, there's no more life.

Forward is the way she wants to move; she's always gone in that direction.

But something keeps her where she is. The pain on the heel of her foot, her gratitude for the sharp rock which makes the pain possible. She looks down at her bare feet. There is blood. She remembers Howard telling her that it wouldn't hurt to be stabbed. What would hurt, he told her, would be the air weaving inside the wound. All of his knowledge came from thick, quickly read spy novels which she read before he did. He never failed to cull some detail she had completely missed. She seems to understand this now.

They had always agreed that they would "go" together, Muriel and Howard. The first to pass into the spirit world would offer some sign to the other that everything was ready, that there were indeed souls moving about, chatting up the novices about life, eternity, the future, ready to solve every last mystery. And the other could come ahead safely, the path having been tested.

"I don't know how I'll go," Howard had once said, "but when I do, I'll be off like a bride's nightie." Eager. Painless. Off.

And Muriel said to this, "Come back just as quick."

Both, when they talked on this subject, were more or less convinced of their immortality.

On the way to the cemetery, her three children and their spouses had heard knocking, three knocks, on the limousine window. As talk of ghosts and spirits shot through the livingroom later, Muriel retired to her room, enervated and confused. Was that it? Why hadn't the rogue knocked up front where she had been sitting, sipping from a mickey of lemon gin with the chauffeur, both of them oozing discussion of the paranormal like it was gossip about those neighbour kids.

She stayed up all night and waited for a cold breeze to pass between the sheets, for Howard's ethereal form to take its place on the futon with a spy novel and drink his absinthe from a cold pewter cup. For him to whisper, "We have known each other forever" and lick her earlobe. It's possible she nodded off once or twice, but not long enough, she figures, to have missed him if he'd come back.

Howard had died as "Fragile" was playing on the car stereo. Muriel had a make-fun way of humming along to Sting because her children thought her too old for him, because she and Howard thought themselves invincible. Howard was amused by how little was expected of you when you were older, by Muriel's hair all bobby-pinned under a kerchief, by their pretend picaresque life, by the fact that Muriel had, over the years, become the one who did all the driving. Even in their fabulous schemes to pull off the perfect heist, Howard charmed someone into handing over riches and Muriel waited out back in the getaway car, her foot gunning the accelerator for practice.

The cortège of cars to the cemetery seemed cruelly similar to the one he had created a few days earlier by slumping over his shoulder belt on the Airport Parkway, the one she had created by not pulling over to the side of the road. A steady stream of lights began to wind around them, a camera flashing over and over for the same still thing as though its subject were irreplaceable. She was reminded of the neon beneath the window in their first hotel room, how they had only noticed its blinking afterward. White, yellow. White, yellow.

Everything had a morbid sense of continuity. Her faculties for one. Her pulse. Howard's timepiece. The notes she had packed in his suitcases for his trip that said I LOVE YOU, DON'T FORGET YOUR PILLS, THINK OF ME IN LACE, CANADA TRUST IN THE YEAR 2000, each on a separate piece of paper she kept now in her sweater pocket, folding and unfolding them. The smell of his pillow and the geography of its creases which she followed to the ends with her fingertips, trying not to disturb ridges and dips. Sting's voice, scratching at the air, over and over, in an effort to rise above the high volume she kept it set at.

The rogue isn't coming back, she thinks. She figures he's thinking he can make it up to her later. Muriel became antsy when she didn't get her way, but Howard always placated her with a charming smile that displayed two gold teeth, and with a playful pat on the behind, or an erection pressed like an offering at the base of her spine. Howard had his reasons, silly and sentimental, and he was able to make her accept them because Howard had a way of making anything make sense.

As a widow, she knows a sadness too heavy for the body and it seeps out into the land, changing its colours and sounds, its smells too. There is no urgency out there. Even the bird overhead has only to keep its wings outstretched to keep moving. She watches everything formally and says out loud in the same tone, "Howard, we have known each other forever." There is urgency in her voice when she adds, "Haven't we?"

She realizes she is supposed to wait. She has no talent for it. Sometimes a jab of panic causes a sudden alertness, but it cannot thrive before land so lifeless and dull, and dissolves like an unfed obsession. She presses the balls of her feet into the hard cold earth, the sharpness of the place where she is standing. The land, like this, lies supine beneath her like something over which she has power, like Howard's body when she got on top of it and rode him as though she were still young. The wind on her face is like Howard's breath, his desire for her, desperate and relentless. She can feel blood, warm and ticklish as come, racing through her; it leaks out slowly, matching the stance of an old woman affecting stillness, the slow lines of her skin.

Any shift in rhythm, any shift at all, and she'll be tempted to walk in the direction she and Howard had rehearsed.

❖

The very first time Constance makes it past the front porch into Muriel's house, Muriel is snipping Howard out of all the family photographs. Sitting primly in the family room, Muriel cuts. Odd and mottled body parts fall and surround her feet. She snip-snips like a carnivore, her scissors glinting in the sunlight like large ready teeth. She works too quickly and cuts the tip of her left thumb, squeals, staunches the blood with her lips.

"Grab yourself a pair," she instructs happily, "this is a party!"

Constance removes her black leather jacket and plunks herself indifferently next to Muriel.

"Look at him in this one," Muriel exclaims, "he has hair!"

She confides to Constance that when she met him his head was bounteous with curls, that she used to search through them in the foolish hope that the meaning of life would be revealed to her. He had plumbed the depths of her body the way she had plumbed the depth of his curls, with a faith that sometimes turned to fear, and a fear that sometimes turned to faith.

She notices Constance's lips are black, also her nails. "That's not a way to walk around," Muriel says. "Not where I come from, young lady."

Muriel tears a picture of her and Howard in half, tosses Howard in the Howard heap. "I'm doing my best to forget."

"Before I ran away I turfed all the pictures of my parents. They could be living next door and I wouldn't even know them," Constance admits matter-of-factly.

"This one I'll keep," Muriel says and holds up a picture of Howard who is sitting, she explains, at Ian Fleming's writing table in Montserrat, where they'd gone to pull themselves together after their first grandchild was born. Muriel's eyes begin to water and she places the picture face down on the coffee table. "That man. He never once went back on his word."

"Let's do the groceries. I'll let you live dangerously this time and buy some Häagen-Dazs." Constance has been paid by Muriel's oldest son, in addition to what Muriel already pays her, to keep Muriel from wallowing.

Muriel pays Constance's roommates too, though not as much or as often as she pays Constance. Even though they live next to Muriel, they have turned out to be about as conscientious as Howard gave them credit for. John puts the garbage out too early and the animals make a mess of it all over the street and front lawn. Billy tries to make psychedelic designs with the lawnmower and by the time the grass gets cut, it needs to be cut again. Rob and Cal, who are supposed to take turns washing her car, blast Metallica out their windows and wait for the Food Cupboard to deliver them the milk that goes with their Sugar Pops and cartoons. They are all runaways, drop-outs who pool their welfare checks to pay rent so they won't be sent back to what they ran away from or dropped out of.

Muriel has just come in from throwing a tantrum on the psychedelic lawn and Constance has just been wakened to go over and calm her.

Constance never seemed to fit into the puzzle Muriel and Howard made of them all. She would sit by herself on the back porch for hours on end and watch the sparrows twitter all along the clothesline. It turns out her budgie, pounced on by one of Bill's cats, lay buried at her feet inside a Kentucky Fried Chicken box. Muriel, upon discovering the motive for her relentless brooding, offered her a job and to buy her another pet. She refused both, until Howard died, and then she accepted the job, claiming she had nothing better to do anyway.

Together, Muriel and Constance make their way to the Asten Martin parked in the driveway. Constance has her three-sixty-five and Muriel lets her drive. Rob is outside on his own porch, drinking beer and smoking a cigarette. A young thing in a bikini sits on his knee. He waves to Muriel, flashes the young girl's breasts, tries to insert his hand down the front of her pants, but she squirms off him, giggling.

By Howard's timepiece it is nine o'clock in the morning.

Constance says the girl is a whore and a slut. Muriel, laughing, tells her there is no such thing, but she is flustered, off balance again.

"There's a lot I could teach you if I planned to stay around that long. About the birds and the bees, I mean." Muriel says this when they come to the yield sign in front of the Quickie store.

Constance comes to a full stop. "Is there?"

"Since your mother is not here to tell you, I will tell you. From time immemorial things between a man and a woman have never changed and they never will. It hurts like Hell the first time, but not so much you won't want to try it again. You can get by on very little and learn as you go, if there's humour and if there's tenderness."

As they drive, Constance tells Muriel she didn't feel a thing the first four times. One month she got behind in the rent and the guys said they'd let it slide if they could each have a go at screwing her.

"What happened to my hymen? Where did it go? I didn't feel a thing. I remember I slammed right on top of the bar that ran across that bike I stole from that kid down the street. I'm pretty sure that's it. And I'm pretty sure it was those assholes who killed my bird because I wasn't a very good fuck. They said they might as well have been drilling a corpse for all the participating I did."

Constance, turning left, almost veers into oncoming traffic in the wrong lane.

"Oh," Muriel says. "Oh dear." This is something she would have kept from Howard, the way she kept from him the endings of books so that he'd keep asking and she'd keep refusing and things just wouldn't end. He would have gone next door and hung those boys up by their feet. She could hear him now. "The body of woman is a gift. You forget that again, I'll forget my warning at home."

Muriel wonders what to do next.

"Maybe there's a thing or two I could teach *you*," Constance says right after putting the car in park.

They do the groceries quickly and although Muriel is still feeling flustered, she convinces Constance to zip through the pet store. She won't take no for an answer today. She wants to buy Constance something to keep her company because, as she says, "It won't be long now."

"Pets die," Constance reminds her, "unless an elephant or a whale is what you have in mind."

"A little hamster would be nice. They run on a wheel all night long and keep everyone awake."

At the entrance to Little Kritters, a slew of dwarf rabbits is being petted by children. One little girl yanks a rabbit's ear, the one asleep in the water bowl. Muriel thinks this is the one Constance will choose after making a show of inspecting the others.

There are German Shepherd puppies frolicking behind a rectangle of glass, guinea pigs, mice, rats, lizards. A huge snake stares, its body a wind-up of concentric circles like the bun at the back of the salesgirl's head. Half the animals are awake; half are asleep. It seems to be a well-proportioned thing, a balance Muriel would, inexplicably, like to upset. She taps on the glass that separates her from all the animals along the bottom row, defying instructions printed on a card.

She knuckles an aquarium and the fish inside veers suddenly away. Maybe Constance would consider a piranha.

"What about one of these?" Constance asks. Her posture is indifferent and her tone is flippant.

Constance is standing in front of a cage of chain-link fence which stretches three feet above her head. Inside, a blue and gold macaw, which must be the male because it's showier, has its beak buried in an umbrella cockatoo's behind. For several minutes its head goes back and forth in her feathers there and the cockatoo raises no obvious objections. Imperiously then, their beaks open and begin to weave around each other, their black tongues frantically trying to touch. They flicker and suck. Customers have gathered and are mesmerized. Nothing moves except the birds.

Muriel is stirring between her legs. She thinks it is the most beautifully erotic thing she has ever seen and feels an inkling of privilege, though she couldn't say why. Maybe it's because Constance's face has softened for a second, or that she has witnessed, in spite of life, that there is tenderness in love, if not eternity.

The salesgirl says their names are ...

But the names are lost in the crumpling of Muriel's body as it falls to the floor.

❖

When Muriel comes to, she wonders why her tongue is sticking out of her mouth and why she can't control it and express her many questions and fears. The photograph of Howard in Montserrat sits lonesomely on her dressing table beside a vase full of impatiens picked, no doubt, from her garden. Constance is reading in the corner on Howard's futon. The bed Muriel lies in has a silver bar alongside it. It isn't hers and this is not her room.

Constance comes to her directly when she tries, and fails, to get out of bed.

"I'll tell you again," she practically sings. "You are at the

Central Park Lodge. You have had a stroke. You may not remember this."

Muriel thinks. She concentrates on remembering by remembering herself in the field after Howard died. Next she comes up with a picture of herself drinking hot coffee through a straw. She sees Constance sitting on the futon and wonders why she doesn't ever seem to go home — she must have a family that misses her. A woman walks the halls, watching her watch. A man sneaks into her room. He lifts her nightie, fondles her breasts, pinches her nipples. Is that you, Rob, she wonders. He licks her crooked tongue as though it were a popsicle and she lets him. It might make Howard jealous.

One whole side of her is useless anyway, the left, the side her heart is on.

Now that she remembers, she would like to forget.

The room is a sullen cream colour with nothing to look at but a sullen cream-coloured floor she could crack her skull on, have it over and done with. She hasn't the strength to do things for herself. Constance has followed her eyes, her ideas, and says, "I know it's hard to swallow, but it'll get better, you'll see."

It sounds like, "Once you hit bottom, there's nowhere to go but up." This was something Howard had said to persuade her to sleep with him before they were married. Bottom was the scoundrel who'd just two-timed on her and left her for broken, and up was the way of Howard's erection, where he promised to take her with it. He pressed it against her behind as she stood with her back to him, and she pretended to be shocked.

The scoundrel — she could not remember his name — sat outside City Hall in his car the day she married Howard. She had never given him another thought until now. Howard tossed him the bridal bouquet, dipped Muriel by the hood ornament and kissed her in the brash French style. How that man liked to kiss with his tongue.

On their wedding night they were supposed to drive to

Niagara Falls. They made it as far as the Château Laurier, ten blocks from the reception hall. She was to slip into the bathroom, have a long luxurious bath and emerge in a white peignoir while Howard waited and tried to imagine what a vision she would be. The salesgirl had said, "So dear and I bet it doesn't stay on for more than two minutes. You'll be lucky if it stays in one piece." And she ought to know, she had said, because she'd been in the business thirty years and thirty years wasn't long enough for anything to change.

Howard carried her over the threshold and deposited her diagonally on the bed. They didn't turn down the sheets. He flung her panties over a lampshade; she was still in her going away dress, a hat still on her head. Over scrambled eggs and a martini, he declared that he loved her and that she would never be rid of him. They had that bath together and with soapy kisses he washed her spine, then the long, infinite line of her palm.

Constance holds her hand, doesn't say anything, just smiles. Muriel tries to speak, but the words come out in blobs of sound that aren't anything like the voice she's accustomed to in her own head. Nothing in her experience has prepared her to adjust to living without the insulation of Howard. Life without him is not even recognizable. She is ready to move forward, only where is he, what could be keeping him.

"You've had a stroke," Constance says, "and some little ones since then. Don't get all worked up again."

Muriel grunts as loudly as she can and indicates, charade-like, that she wants a pen. Constance fishes one out of her back jean pocket and gives Muriel the white sheet of the bed to write on. With her right hand, Muriel scribbles, when will I die?

"When I say."

When? Muriel makes a W in the air.

"Not yet."

She makes another W.

"Just give me twenty years to get my act together. Stick around and teach me things. Okay?"

Muriel attempts to make another W and her hand slams against the bar of the bed.

"I liked the birds. I bought the birds. The birds'll be good company, I want you to know."

Pets die. What happened to my hymen? Let's do the groceries.

Howard, finally, is sitting on his futon. He is dressed casually, is tanned, seems out of breath as though he's been hurrying to get here on time. The book he's pretending to read is upside down and he gives Muriel a look. The look says he has skipped ahead to the end without reading the middle and could she please fill him in? She hasn't decided whether or not to spoil things for him, but teases, "So, you want to know how it all turns out?"

"I know," he says. "I tried to tell you only you weren't listening."

"I am now."

He takes her by the hand and they begin to waltz together in the field behind their house. The teenagers have their music blaring, but Howard sings "Fragile" right into her ear so they won't be bothered by it.

Constance waves from her back porch, a blaze of bird on each of her shoulders. The macaw and the cockatoo.

"Look at him in this one," Muriel calls out, "he has hair!"

Constance laughs and laughs. Muriel's words are as clear as anything she's ever heard her say and go soaring above her, the weeping willows, the sky.

Howard slips his tongue playfully into Muriel's mouth, showing off. He says what she's been waiting all this time for him to say and he says it without using one word.

Drama Junkies

EVERY LAST ONE OF THEM IS HERE. MY WIFE JULIA, MY MOTHER-in-law Nora, my step-daughter Jewel. Johanne is here with her husband, Jared with his wife, Joe Junior with his pet snake Cubbins coiled up in the pocket of his windbreaker. The whole famn damily, as they say, side by each for the unparallelled, but not unexpected crisis.

It has taken less than an hour to mobilize the forces and assemble. Julia gave her mother a dingle right after I told her what happened, then this one called that one, that one called this one; dominoes tipping against dominoes until the last of them toppled.

I'm here too, with garbage bags and twist ties stuffed in the pockets of my coveralls. Oh and Hank, let us not forget Hank, the guy from Mobile Autoglass with a brand new windshield to replace the one broken by the man we are all supposed to dread and fear.

"What you're saying is," Hank says as he appears to be smoothing the windshield with his palm. He is looking directly at Nora whose face by now is blanched and otherworldly from the shock of what her ex-husband has sunk to. "What you're saying is, this was no Act of God. You've got a lunatic on your hands. That is what you're saying, Ma'am?"

Up until now I'm the one who's done the important talking. Let's not forget this happened to me and that I'm the one who's been doing his level best to take care of the situation. Nora hasn't uttered one word yet. She reaches into her purse for her inhaler, forces a moment's reprieve into her lungs. She's about to speak, decides not to.

"You've got to see it to believe it." I toss my two cents in again, not to be outdone by the fact that I'm the newest member of this family, married to Nora's daughter Julia only three months. "This man has caused so much damage nobody can see straight."

"Know the type. Know it well," Hank says, eyeing me in the most peculiar fashion.

Showboat that he is, Hank struts over to the mound of crushed glass, kneels and scoops some into his bare hands. He tilts his palms downward abruptly, as though he is closing a very fine book. The glass cascades without so much as a tinkle, and looking around I can tell what all of them are thinking. With the bull's head for a belt buckle, Hank's got horns in a place you wouldn't want to be caught staring. Hank, with the pockmarked face and craters so huge you could hide in them, is a magician; a handyman of legerdemain; a prize of prestidigitation; a jack-of-all-trades.

Two hands now on a razor, slicing through glue and rubber, prying the demolished windshield from my Mazda 323, Hank is going to make all of this disappear. Hank is going to make it all better.

Sadly, there is nothing that Hank can do about the slashed

tires, but his years of experience with this sort of thing put him in the best possible position to dispense advice. We are expected to be grateful for his telling us up front. Too many times, he has seen the same kind of damage caused by the same kind of lunatic. The Hamiltons have to take cover outside the lunatic's house, armed with crowbars and baseball bats, this is what they have to do. "Keep your eyes peeled. And stay pumped," Hank counsels. "Fight fire with fire." They are told to clobber the sucker, if he shows himself, right across the windpipe; they are told to fix his wagon same as he fixed theirs.

"*My* wagon," I correct him. "It was *my* bloody wagon. And that's not the way to handle things."

"He won't know what hit him," Hank smiles proudly and they all know Hank's right because the same thing, minus the crowbars and baseball bats, has just happened to them. "The element of surprise is a powerful weapon."

Glass had flown in every direction when Julia's father surprised me by throwing a rock at my car. A rock the size of my fist flew through the windshield to the right of the steering wheel, pursued by a comet of glass beads, some of which landed in my hair. I'm still worried there's glass inside the car, in places too tough to see.

I know what the man is capable of because you don't sign up with this family without hearing the horror stories. So, the instant the boulder hit I could not keep, albeit reluctantly, from checking my ribcage for blood and a bullet hole.

In my family we reminisce about the time we rented a cottage in Calabogie, the time Dawn sat on the frog and it euphemistically croaked, the birthday my mother baked me a layered cake and forgot to remove the aluminum foil in between. "What a freakish feeling filled our fillings!" we tongue-twister-sang around the campfire. The way my family compares happy memories, my wife and my in-laws compare scars, emotional as well as physical. Who has the biggest and who has the deepest, and who do you think's to blame?

After Mr. Hamilton threw the boulder and slashed the tires, he left a note. Since I refused to roll down the window for the hand-to-hand delivery, he impaled it on the antenna. In my shock I'd forgotten about it, but Johanne points it out, inquiring as to its nature. I read it, first to myself, then in excerpts to the family.

"Oh," says Johanne after I'm finished reading, "thought for a second it might be a flag of surrender."

The note demands access to Jewel. Access, Hamilton calls it. He is putting us on notice — Jewel is his beneficiary, the trustee of his will, which can be located in the top left hand drawer of his desk. What money he has to bequeath is anybody's guess, since he's been collecting disability for the last three years and as far as anybody knows he's still in hock to the government for thousands of dollars in back taxes.

None of the other Hamiltons had better dare show up at his funeral which, I guess, we are to understand from the note, is imminent. But if they want to heal the rift and let go of their petty resentment, he will be Christian enough to listen. That's just the kind of man he is. The only one who'll be allowed to view him in his casket, however, is Jewel. For Jewel, his special trinket, he has asked to be decked out in his blue pinstripe suit with a snapdragon in the lapel.

"Is this guy for real?" I say, laughing out aloud, because for me, this is the point where you can stop feeling sorry for the man, the point where it gets so silly you can write him off altogether, like my windshield. Who does he think's going to dress him, in a world filled with the casualties of all his failed relationships? I don't figure there's anyone he could pay to do that job.

But the whole family ignores me, arguing amongst themselves, puzzling with great concern over the definition of a snapdragon. Jared says it's a reptile like Cubbins whose poison has no known antidote. Julia says that no, no, she thinks it's a martial art thing, what you might call an insignia.

"You know Dad and his karate."

Hank clears his throat, speaks up that this is likely. Just from the little he's heard so far, it stands to reason that a man like Hamilton would need a way to advertise to others just who he is and what he belongs to. A man resorts to crazy tactics when he's got nothing left to lose. "Safety in numbers, isn't that what I told you?"

"I'm with Hank," I hear.

Someone says, "Hank is right."

I move to the side and start to clean up what glass Hank has piled in a mound in the parking lot, sweeping with my steel toe, sweeping the pile of shards out of my sight. What I wouldn't give to spend a long quiet evening, just me, Julia and Jewel for once, then a long quiet night, when I can watch them sleep. But, oh no, this is not to be. It is supper time. Make way, y'all, because it is Hamilton time!

Julia has been cooking all afternoon and there's plenty for everyone. Hurray. Even for Hank whom she invites to join us without running it by me first. There *is* a God in Heaven because Hank declines and Nora leads her looking-over-their-shoulders brood indoors. Even Jared, who weighs over three hundred pounds and who could snap his father in half, has a flushed face and the wild awake eyes of a terrified baby. I won't bother to hassle him about it because if he is twice the size of his father, he's got to be three times the size of me.

In a couple of minutes, Hank approaches, looking me right in the eye. It occurs to me I'm looking at a man who probably hunts deer with a crossbow, just for the sport of watching the animals dart away with lungfuls of blood.

"That just about wraps up my end," he says, writing up an invoice, then squeezing my hand tight until my skin is pasted to his callouses. "I guess the rest is up to you. You *do* have insurance, right?"

❖

"Supper!" Julia bellows out the front door. "Come on, Doug, supper!"

Since one o'clock in the afternoon pork chops have been softening, turning to mush, in the pressure cooker. In many ways Julia is not like the other Hamiltons, yet in this way, with her compulsion to be overly cautious, she is exactly the same. For this reason, most of what I eat isn't edible, which for the time being, until I get things under control, is an acceptable situation. Part of my strategy stems from the reasoning: acknowledge the reality of something, and it tends to become real.

You will eat it, you will like it, you will say so.

I sing this like a refrain as I twirl the garbage bag and tie it up. To the degree I am enthusiastic, to say that I love her cooking may be the difference between a pleasant, peaceable meal and an all-out war about the bind we're in financially, about Jewel's Social Studies project which comes up again and again, about my first wife who has been (by Jewel) and who will be (by Jewel) referred to as Her Haughtiness, the Galloping Gourmet, also a subject which comes up again and again.

"Why do you love me?" Julia always wants to know, on the prowl for specifics here.

"Because I just *do*," is what I tell her.

I tote the garbage bag inside, stopping to wash my hands at the kitchen sink because I have nicked myself on the shards.

A Band-Aid between my thumb and index, I head downstairs to see where everybody's gotten to. They're all sitting on the sofas with plates on their laps, glued to the Trial Of The Century, so-called, on television. Each of them has been following it religiously since day one.

Julia is walking around with a pot and ladle, pouring Bernaise sauce over everybody's meat, trying to explain as she goes the concept of genetic fingerprinting — DNA.

"Doomed by genetics. That's it and that's all," says Julia, which launches them into a mini-discussion over the nature versus nurture issue. Nora seems saddened by her children's quickly reached consensus that they have been handed a double whammy — bad genes *and* bad upbringing, but the rest of them are animated, they are positively pulsing, like a transplant heart in the hand of a surgeon. Christ almighty, Joe Junior is crooning to his snake, syncopating the conversation with the karate chops of his air drumming.

Jewel, trailing far behind Julia, offers up the pepper mill to blacken everybody's creamy white potatoes, saying *guilty* with every grind.

"You make a better door than a window," Jared says, shoving her in front of Nora.

"No pepper for her, darling, but you could get Gramma a cold glass of water," says Joe Junior.

"Would you like a glass of water?" I ask Nora, playing the part of host and trying to get on her good side. Nora is not enchanted with me because I deigned to love another woman before her daughter Julia. She says this constitutes adultery no matter which way you cut it and never mind that another man knocked Julia up and split from the responsibility. Convenient the way some people overlook the truth, is what I say.

"She would kill for a glass of water," says Johanne. "Wouldn't you, Mother?"

"Any other takers while I'm up?"

On the tube, our notorious defendant is flanked by five lawyers wearing suits at least as pricey as his own. The slew of them look like rats with beady eyes and quick, alert body shifts. Nobody answers me. All Hamilton eyes are riveted once again to the trial which, even the pundits agree, is in the slow, dull phase.

And you can be sure there is no dispute about *this* amongst the Hamiltons: it was *much* more interesting at the beginning of the case when pictures were shown and tapes played. What they're watching now is a big time bore. Mercifully, at any moment, you never know when, things will pick up and the lawyers will start to show blood instead of just plain talk about it. It hasn't taken me too long to figure out that the Hamiltons (junkies, every last one of them) and their spouses, who may as well be Hamiltons, live for moments like these.

Sure enough, as if on cue, the splendid moment is delivered, a moment to fix on and shoot deep into their veins. Jared's wife Kat blurts out that there is so much unpredictable craziness out there, that she feels we must take measures to protect ourselves against it. Unlisted phone numbers for a start. Barricaded doors. State of the art security systems. It does not seem foolish or extreme in the least to her that everybody give up their places in town and move together into a big, rambling house in the country. She can hardly sleep a wink at night just imagining what this crazy man is likely to do next. For a moment I stop to ask myself which crazy man she is talking about. By now I have been introduced to several.

Voices rise as though hastening skyward up a rickety ladder. Voices speed up as though prodded with electricity. The Hamiltons are positively wired now, stoned out of their trees. Possibilities ricochet around the room, escalating in terror until Nora hears Jewel sobbing in the corner and calls for everyone's attention by pointing. Jewel is facing the corner where two walls of knotty pine converge, her arms wrapped around herself in a hug. What's the matter! What's the matter, they want to know, as if it could hold a candle to earlier events. They trample each other with sudden alarm in their eagerness to touch her skin and find out.

"What, Jewel, what?" Julia asks. "Tell Mommy."

Jewel wants to know if she will be forced to see her grandfather's dead body if she doesn't feel like it. She wants to know if the snapdragon has fangs.

❖

The Judge has called a recess in the trial and Jewel, in the interim, is being allowed to present the family tree she traced for school. Anything to keep her mind off her troubles. This tree is so well-coloured, you can get slivers from looking at the bark, the branches so arthritic you can feel ache in all your joints. You can smell and taste the luscious red apples strewn along the ground of this cardboard project and have your mouth water. That is if you're not put off by the clouds raining down fake red blood, blood spilling through two generations of Hamiltons.

What you cannot see unless you know it's there is the F given by her teacher Mrs. Roy. Mrs. Roy called to tell Julia and me it wasn't that Jewel hadn't made an impressive beginning, just that she hadn't taken things far enough. It is common knowledge, she said, that in a genealogy most of the tree is supposed to be dead. Mrs. Roy does not share Jewel's interest in the distaff side of her family, nor in the old man whose face Jewel has gruesomely woven into the bark. Mrs. Roy wants to see the Courteau ancestors of Jewel's father's side, the spear side, emphasized and stretched all the way back to Europe. Jewel, we were told decisively, is not allowed to be an apple core in an old man's mouth.

Julia tells them about Mrs. Roy. "The woman refuses to back down, so Doug and I are taking it up with the School Board."

"*Julia* is taking it up with the School Board," I say. "*I* am pitching for Jewel to make this project a fun thing. I told her I'd help. Drive her to the library, drive her to the cemetery to find names and dates, help her get hold of baptism, marriage and death certificates, whatever she needs to do things the proper way. I don't think it's healthy for a ten-year-old to be taking things so seriously. I'm new to this step-father business, but I think a ten-year-old ought to be out there doing ten-year-old things. Like when I was a kid."

"We have to street-proof her. She's a Hamilton through and through," says Julia, "and there's no running away from that." With the dazed and mellow look of addicts, they nod or murmur assent. Julia is preaching to the converted.

"Listen, I'm sorry. That's not what I meant to say." I have found that sometimes it's better to just leave well enough alone, especially when Julia is casting me the evil eye. "Anyone up for a game of Rumoli? Come on, Jewel, I'll spot you a dollar."

I am told bluntly, but politely, that this is not the time to play games. The Hamiltons will forgive my insensitivity since I haven't been around long enough to know any better and since I grew up with all the advantages, especially and enviably the one of ordinariness and normalcy. They smirk. How else would someone in my shoes react? It's quite understandable, they scoff. It's quite predictable.

Jared, not so polite, advises me to shut my trap and mind my own beeswax. "When it comes to Hamilton business, I hate to say this," he says, "you don't know your ass from a hole in the ground."

My blood boiling, I grab Jewel by the hand and lead her up

to the kitchen. The deck of cards is lying on the top of the fridge beside the Job Jar which is filled with yellow stickies. Fix the Breadmaker; Fix the Starter on the Barbecue; Fix Every Goddamned Thing that is Broken. Without taking the time to remove the Jokers, I shuffle furiously and deal out the cards.

"You can't play Rumoli with two people," I explain to her. "We're going to have to play War."

Now I am spitefully slapping down Aces over tens, eights over twos, Jacks over fives and piling my winnings high in front of me. I am staying pumped and keeping my eyes peeled on Jewel's piddly stack, just waiting to steal it with a card that matches.

"Now we're having some fun eh, Doll?" I say, feeling the rush.

The phone rings. We are in the middle of a double war. Eight times, eleven times, seventeen times. I yank the phone off the wall and press it to my ear. Julia has picked up at the same time downstairs. Her father is on the line, calling from the trauma ward of the hospital, he says, with severe chest pains. A woman who is supposed to be a nurse comes on to confirm this, then hands the call back to Hamilton. I say *supposed* because she mispronounces infarction. Infraction is the word she uses instead.

"This is your last chance. Bring her to me or else."

"Or else what?" Julia asks.

"I'll leave *that* to your fertile imagination."

"Come on by." I sound like Bob Barker now from *The Price Is Right*, extending this invitation in the same tone as I save for my best friends, warm and heartfelt. "I mean it. Don't be a stranger." Then I start to hammer the phone into the wall with louder and louder thuds.

"Fucking Jesus!" Julia yells. "Fucking, fucking, fucking Jesus," she chants to the rhythm of my hammering.

I throw the phone and race to the bottom of the stairs. Julia is sitting in the Lazy-Boy with the phone in her lap and the first thing I think of is a newborn with umbilical cord wrapped around its neck. We have been trying to get pregnant for a year and here it is, a child of our own, white and strangled and helpless in her legs.

Julia has asked me what I would like to name our boy or girl. Would I like to continue the tradition of J names or would I prefer to name our children after me? In her book *What Shall We Name The Baby?* Douglas means dweller by the dark stream. "Isn't that a delicious thing to know?" she asks. With no idea what she wants or expects from me, I say we'll cross that bridge when we come to it.

"Maybe we should go?" Julia says to her family. "You think we should? Just think if it's for real. How would we live with ourselves?"

"I'll give you three reasons not to." This is me talking. "I love you. You're not going. I won't let you."

"Why do you love me?" she asks, but she's not really asking here, she's testing me again. "Because of my great good looks or is it something else? Go on, Doug, tell me for once. Nail it down for all of us."

Within a couple of minutes, it's a complete shambles down here. Screaming, crying, fighting, swearing, Nora gasping for breath. I run into the unfinished part of the basement and find myself a baseball bat. I unplug the TV, swing the bat right into it.

They are quiet but, something tells me, largely unchanged. Looking at them, I ask myself what it will take. I ask myself why I married this family, because marry the whole crew I did, *and* all their history, *and* all that history's future.

The night Julia proposed, I said yes, I would be honoured. She said, "Good. Because you haven't lived until you've almost died. You'll see. You're not attracted to the meaning of my pain as much as you are to the sensation." She could be so enigmatic sometimes, but here was a lethal combination, me and a woman playing hard to get.

I told her I was attracted to the way she could use nonsense and foul language with perfect impunity. And, for a joke, because she was very good in bed. She slapped my face, which left me speechless. Until now.

"Listen carefully," I tell them, my eyes fixed on Julia whose eyes are not yet fixed on me, "because I'm only going to say this once. This is what we're going to do."

Jewel who has come to join the unfolding drama treads closer and I notice she's in her bare feet. I yank her by the wrist to stop her dead before she cuts herself, but when she points at the floor, there isn't a speck of glass visible to the naked eye. The tube has imploded. Every last piece of glass has been sucked inside. It's somehow like I forced the defendant to open his mouth and swallow every contemptible thing this world has ever known.

PATRICIA NOLAN is a writer and teacher of creative writing. Her work has appeared in *Quarry, Canadian Fiction, The Capilano Review, Event, University of Windsor Review, Fiddlehead, Blood & Aphorisms, The Malahat Review, Grain, Prism International* and *Best Canadian Stories*. She lives in Kanata, Ontario.

POLESTAR FIRST FICTION

The Polestar First Fiction series celebrates the first published book of fiction — short stories or novel — of a Canadian writer. Polestar is committed to supporting new writers, and contributing to North America's dynamic and diverse cultural fabric.

ANNIE
Luanne Armstrong • 1-896095-00-3 • $16.95 CAN / $12.95 USA

••

BROKEN WINDOWS
Patricia Nolan • 1-896095-20-8 • $16.95 CAN / $14.95 USA

••

THE CADILLAC KIND
Maureen Foss • 1-896095-10-0 • $16.95 CAN / $14.95 USA

••

CRAZY SORROW
Susan Bowes • 1-896095-19-4 • $16.95 CAN / $14.95 USA

••

DISTURBING THE PEACE
Caroline Woodward • 0-919591-53-1 • $14.95 CAN / $12.95 USA

••

HEAD COOK AT WEDDINGS AND FUNERALS
Vi Plotnikoff • 0-919591-75-2 • $14.95 CAN / $12.95 USA

••

A HOME IN HASTIE HOLLOW
Robert Sheward • 1-896095-11-9 • $16.95 CAN / $14.95 USA

••

IF HOME IS A PLACE
K.Linda Kivi • 1-896095-02-X • $16.95 CAN / $12.95 USA

••

RAPID TRANSITS AND OTHER STORIES
Holley Rubinsky • 0-919591-56-6 • $12.95 CAN / $10.95 USA

Polestar Book Publishers takes pride in creating books that enrich our understanding and enjoyment of the world, and in introducing discriminating readers to exciting new writers. Whether in prose or poetry, these independent voices illuminate our history, stretch our imaginations, engage our sympathies and evoke the universal through narrations of everyday life.

Polestar titles are available from your local bookseller. For a copy of our complete catalogue — featuring poetry, fiction, fiction for young readers, sports books and provocative non-fiction — please contact us at:

POLESTAR BOOK PUBLISHERS
1011 Commercial Drive, Second Floor
Vancouver, British Columbia
CANADA   V5L 3X1
phone (604) 251-9718 • fax (604) 251-9738